COMMUNITY KILLING

A DI Huws Crime Thriller Book 1 of 3

ANNE ROBERTS

Dedication

I DEDICATE THIS BOOK TO THE MEMORY OF MY LATE HUSBAND MIKE ROBERTS, WRITING AND ALL THINGS CONNECTED WAS HIS THING.

Acknowledgments

THIS BOOK IS FICTION BASED ON FACT, WHICH WILL MAKE ITSELF APPARENT AS THE TALE DEVELOPS. ALL NAMES USED ARE FICTIONAL, BUT MOST PLACES DO EXIST. PEOPLE MAY WELL IMAGINE THAT THEY RECOGNISE THEMSELVES IN THE STORY AND I THANK ALL THE PEOPLE WHO WERE ACTUALLY INVOLVED ALONGSIDE ME IN THE TRUE PARTS OF THE TALE, MY PARENTS AND SISTER AND BUSINESS PARTNER WHO ALSO WITNESSED VARIOUS SCENES FROM THIS BOOK. ALSO HUGE THANKS MUST GO TO MY STEP- GRANDDAUGHTER HAYLEY, YET AGAIN FOR HELPING ME WITH THE MORE TECHNICAL ASPECTS OF BOOK PUBLISHING.

Chapter One

August 2019

"Oh God," mumbled Dyfed as he rolled over and grabbed for his pager, its green light flashing demandingly on the bedside cabinet, the high-pitched alarm sounding, "shit," he whispered unintentionally too loudly as he knocked his mobile phone off the cabinet in his efforts to quieten the pager, it fell with a resounding clatter onto the bare board floor and under the bed, jumping up with more activity than he felt the energy for, he bent to scrabble about under the bed to grab the errant phone, his other hand pushing the off button on the pager.

By nature, he was a night owl and had a tendency to go to bed far too late than was good for him. Flicking through the TV channels with the remote much to Elin his wife's annoyance when he eventually came to bed and insisted on warming his cold feet on hers, always waking her up. Once he had got to sleep however, he slept the sleep of the dead, and a pager alert in the early hours always caused his heart to race as he was abruptly woken.

Stumbling half asleep out of the bedroom trying not to disturb Elin who merely gave a knowing moan and turned over pulling the duvet over her exposed shoulder. He needed a pee before he went anywhere, pulling on the light cord in the bathroom he then pulled on his t- shirt, and socks, he grabbed a pair of trousers out of the laundry basket, threw some water at his face then dialled the Ops room on speed dial as he went down the stairs. He took his time on the stairs, having learnt that rushing down wooden varnished treads in socked feet was not the best of plans. His mouth felt like the bottom of a budgies cage as he asked what and where the job was.

He had questioned himself more than a couple of times over the last few months as to whether he was getting too old for this malarkey, the daytime call-outs were OK, being self-employed, he could always drop tools and go, but it seemed harder and harder with the night time jobs, He needed to look at his lifestyle, or he would be heading for an inevitable heart attack.

Hoover the family Labrador wagged his tail against the kitchen cupboard from his basket in the corner, pleased to see his master but too typically Labrador laid- back-lazy to get up in the dead of night, knowing by now he wouldn't get much of a fuss. Grabbing his car keys, he closed the kitchen door behind him. Dyfed had always kept his overalls on the peg in the utility room for convenience, they were easier to put on before his work boots but the rest of his gear lived in the back of his car, ready wherever he happened to be during the day should his pager demand his immediate reaction.

It had been a busy season so far; the end of July and the beginning of August always seemed to be so on their patch. He had a good team now working alongside him, so could always rely on a reasonable turnout of volunteer's day or night. Ten of them altogether, three old stagers,including himself as one of them, with a fair few years of service and used to all sorts, the others, younger, twenties and thirties and some not yet wise to all the ways of the world, a couple not yet used to the slightly sick sense of humour that emanated out of the older team members. They would learn as time went on that it was purely a self-preserving mechanism employed by many like himself all over the UK that were part of such services.

Over the years on various training courses, he had met a few team members that were significantly older than himself. Some were way over a normal retirement age, who were exactly the same in the sense of humour department. A great percentage of them having become quite cynical and scathing about sea visiting humanity as the years went by, it would happen to the younger ones over time. That fact was a guarantee.

Dyfed, clicked the car fob, the doors unlocking with a soft thud, he opened the boot, grabbed his yellow coat and helmet and put them on, preferring to arrive at the scene fully prepared. He jumped into the driver's seat and started the engine, taking care not to rev and possibly reawakening Elin again. He was a good driver, not that he was legally allowed to break any speed limits in his own car, but then again he nearly always did, most people did, having to be aware of the cloud of red mist that descended and potentially clouded their sensibilities. This was a particular risk at night when he would be alerted by oncoming car lights, however, years of experience had taught him that he needed to keep an eye out for the more nocturnal creatures. Annoyingly he had really messed his van up one night when he hit a dog fox, he still felt guilty at not stopping to check it over. He was convinced that the impact had killed it outright, but on driving back home later there was no sign of it, either it had crawled injured to die somewhere, or somehow it had survived. Mind you, he thought, these modern car bumpers were now so plastic and weak that they withstood no bumping at all.

It was a beautiful moonlit night, that was one consolation, at least it was not raining, and being the end of August it was still warm, he looked at the outside temperature gauge, eighteen degrees, not too bad, almost too warm for his fluorescents, but he also well aware from experience that a long search could also coincide with a change in the weather, the dawn often bringing a breeze, which if combined with tiredness could soon chill you.

The chat with the Ops room had told him to rendezvous at a local meeting point with police officers, just to the south of the village of Allt Goch, this was an area of shore popular at this time of year with visitors, a long stretch of exposed bay, around four miles long from end to end. The terrain varied, from low cliffs and boulders on the east side, to a large expanse of sandy beach, for around a third of its length, where the visitor population tended to stay put with their pop-up beach tents and windbreaks. An area where young children would complain about the distance to the water's edge at low tide, a café and toilets for their convenience, sat at the back of the beach area, adjacent to the narrow road along the foreshore where there was a reasonably large car park. The odd camper van often stayed overnight on the grassy areas overlooking the shore. That however was becoming a bit of an issue locally now, the numbers, the litter and the motorhomes getting stuck on the steep hairpin bends caused friction.

From there on, the beach became wider from the high tide mark to the sea, half of the distance made up of saltings and hundreds of sandy holes, carved out over the years by the tides. Holes that were mostly empty at this time of year, but often filled with brackish seawater after the winter storms, where an onshore wind would push the high tide up towards the low-lying fields close to the shore. The water tended to stay in them once filled, debris fell in and by the spring they tended to smell a bit rank, he had more than once in the darkness of a night search heard his teammates fall into them, especially the ones where the reed grasses and rushes had grown around them and hidden them during the day let alone at night. He had done it himself often enough as a youngster, but knew by now that it was often a case of less speed more progress, or whatever the saying was.

The far end of the beach was technically the estuary mouth where the very mud-silted river emptied itself onto the vast wide expanse of beach, running out of steam as opposed to becoming any more powerful. The only time the river filled significantly was when the spring tides had the north easterlies behind them and pushed the river back from whence it came. This whole area was also pretty treacherous as the tide came in, the beach was so flat and wide, a mile and a half almost from the mean high, to low tide marks, causing the tide to move in at almost running pace. There were always cars being submerged on the Red Wharf bay end of the shore, catching unsuspecting visitors out who had dared to park up too far out.

He supposed it was a bit like the Morecambe sands, where all the poor cocklers got cut off and drowned, he had never been there, but had heard stories from team members from that area that he had met at the training school. Terrible it was by all accounts, the sounds of desperation, prayer and lost hope carrying on the breeze without anyone being able to reach them in time. There was no point whatsoever in Dyfed going to the Coastguard station first, he was nearer to the meeting place than the station. One of the team who lived nearer the station would get the truck and bring it down.

Dyfed was the second of his team to arrive, Aled was already there, he lived a little closer to the rendezvous point than Dyfed, in fact, probably no further than half a mile, virtually walking distance.

Aled farmed his smallholding as well as his 'proper' job, as he called it, which was as a highly respected, self-employed, accountant. Because he largely worked from home, he was always the first to respond to a page call, stating that it gave him much-needed relief from the dreariness of calculations, VAT and Tax accounting. Dyfed doubted that was the reason in the middle of the night.

Dyfed was certain that he preferred his farming role, he was a very dependable man, always calm, particularly good at dealing with the occasional obnoxious person they might across, he had long ago accepted that not everyone was relieved at having been rescued, it depended entirely on how they had got themselves into the particular situation.

The police were already there standing around when he arrived, but only two of them up to then, who had arrived by panda car, it couldn't be anything big kicking off he thought to himself, or there would be more of them there.

Soon he picked up the headlights of a couple more cars coming down the hill towards the beach, one would be the Coastguard truck with all the search gear in and one of the other lads or indeed lass would have followed on in their own car.

He'd been a coastguard for 22 years, feeling confident that he had come across most things, Aled who was already at the beach, had three years on him, and was the Station Officer, the head honcho in other words, Dyfed being the deputy, with no aspirations whatsoever to become the Station Officer himself, too much care and maintenance needed and loads of paperwork which was never top of his agenda, although he was totally willing to help with anything that needed attention.

As a mechanic, he had Elin his wife to do all his bookkeeping and accounts, he just made sure he kept all the invoices and receipts in a box in his workshop office that she took away whenever she popped into the garage. Being a Maths teacher in the local secondary school had its uses but woe betide him if he didn't keep his receipts, or allowed one to sit in the foot well of his car to disintegrate.

There were seven of them now at least, if the search area was this beach as he had been told, Aled may well need to ask the ops room to mobilise a flank team — the next team along the coast, maybe the team each side would be needed if the situation warranted it. They all knew their adjacent patches reasonably well, particularly in the daytime but the night was a different story altogether.

Most of the team were kitted out quickly, they were well practised. Yellows, helmets, life jackets over their coats as per rules and a few of them with a small first aid kit slung over their shoulders. Torches in hand fully charged. A couple of them would have some Mars bars in their pockets-just in case it was a long job. The uniform as such was not the most comfortable to wear, sweat inducing at the best of times, not the easiest of clothing to move about in with any athletic dexterity, and tonight would be no different.

Aled was talking to the Police, he stepped across to make sure they were all singing from the same hymn sheet with the right information. Sometimes the police were a little sparse with the information they gave out, occasionally imparting as little as possible to get the job done, for instance-'missing male, last seen at so-and-so and seen walking towards so-and-so,' however tonight was very different. The policeman in charge called them all together for their briefing. He wanted them to contribute their own search plan and expertise.

Sarah Jones, last seen at four pm having walked out of her home after a row with her parents, over her relationship with a lad they believed was very much beneath her social status. She was only fifteen and recently the sparks had been flying at home, when her school had told them at the end of the summer term that she had been absent frequently. The relationship had come to light and the rows had started, particularly between her father and herself.

The parents had issued the police with a good description, and unusually, the police had a recent photo that was shared around for the team to see. They rarely got to see a picture of the missing person.

In most cases where young persons were reported missing, the parents would have covered all bases themselves before reporting their child missing , and often the Coastguard teams were not alerted until the said child had been missing for twenty-four hours or more, by the time all family members and friends had been grilled and those lines of enquiry exhausted, the police were alerted, at this point by a very distressed family member. Sadly at this point there had already been time for them to be well away if that was indeed their plan.

The parents had not got a phone number for the boyfriend, but on naming him, he was known to the police, petty burglaries mainly, but was also known to dabble at the fringes of the world of hard drugs. Not a major player or supplier, but a wanabee. He had already been turfed out of his bed at two am but disappointingly there was no evidence of Sarah having spent the evening with him. Most worryingly, being twenty-seven, he denied any liaison with Sarah beyond hanging out with her and her mates a few times. This according to the girls father was a blatant lie.

More information was dished out, the clothes she was last seen in, the style she had her hair, when she stormed out, a pony tail tied low down at the nape of her neck, she had a pair of silver loop earrings in her ears, and much to her parent's dislike, a nose stud. However, the most important part of the information came at the end, Sarah was diabetic and as she had grown up into her teenage years had become disdainful and worryingly neglectful, of her life-long condition and tried her best to ignore it. As far as her parents were concerned, she had left the house with no money, no snacks, and most importantly, her testing kit was on her chest of drawers. By now her blood sugar could be critically low and in danger of causing a hypoglycaemic episode, this was the main reason the police had responded so quickly as opposed to their occasional, "Let's give them twenty-four hours".

Chapter Two

"CAN YOU GATHER AROUND FOR A MINUTE?" asked Aled. He cleared his throat before continuing. By now he had asked the ops room via landline for more information regards tide times and had been told that high tide was at six-thirty am. It was currently three forty-five am, so they had a bit of time to make sure they covered the main beach area before the tide covered it. Day break would be roughly five-thirty am, but the fact that the expanse of beach covered ten square flat miles, persuaded a forward thinking Aled to ask the Ops room to page the flank teams so that they could conduct at least a hasty search of the area before high tide, a more concentrated grid search could be carried out later on when there were more boots on the ground. It would take a while for the teams to get there, so Aled needed to organise the team of volunteers that were already there and get them started.

"Ok, let's get you splitting into three teams for the moment, with John staying with the truck and maintaining comms, you also are fully aware that the radio comms are rarely brilliant in this area, so make sure you have your mobile phones at hand too. Don't overdo the radio stuff, and clog the channel as there will eventually be a fair few of us out here. The young lady's mobile has been pinged to this area but now the tracing has been lost, so she has either taken the sim out or God forbid, something has happened to her and her phone. Please report obs normal as a welfare check every twenty minutes. Her mates have somehow got wind that she was over this way, so keep an eye out, that if any of them are doing their own thing, that they are aware of the tide and any soft sand areas, we don't want it becoming a mud rescue job as well. "It might help to try to limit the number of public involved in case we have to send the SARDA dogs through later, though no decision has been made to call them out yet and in reality if we have been traipsing our scent through, it may potentially not be sensible. They are also mobilising the inland search and rescue team too. Has anyone bought any chocolate with them?"

"I have," said Ceri.

"You know me boss, always prepared for a long job and thinking of my belly."

"OK," said Aled ignoring her attempt at humour.

"If we find her pretty soon, we can get something sweet down her as long as she is conscious, so just remember your first aid protocols, recovery position, warmth and all that, so don't eat the chocolate Ceri."

"Yup OK," yawned Ceri, still half asleep it seemed, probably had a late night, as the youth of today seemed to do.

Dyfed was paired with David, David was the only English member of the team, being a very welsh rural area, most of the locals were first language welsh, they always spoke welsh to each other, but when David was present, English was spoken, largely out of good manners. David was a secondary school teacher in the local comprehensive school five miles outside the village of Allt Goch, most of the local children were bussed there and back daily. David was easy to chat to. He was, as part of his employment at the school, desperately making great efforts to learn the language.

Dyfed always enjoyed their conversations; it was good to have intelligent topics beyond football and rugby, which other than women, and farting competitions was the daily topic of conversation between the two lads he employed at the workshop. He did not want to even imagine that he could have been as crass himself at that age.

By now there was a slight hint of light to the east, but not enough to see clearly without their torches. The three teams were spaced at intervals across the width of the bay, he could see the torch lights of his colleagues who were making regular sweeps around themselves, looking a little like mini lighthouses in the distance. It was an important part of searching. Never just look ahead and to both sides, making sure that you regularly checked where you had been too. It was easy to miss someone huddled behind a large boulder that you were walking past.

Aled and Michael had ended up nearest the sea, aware all the time of the incoming tide and also aware of all the little gulley's and dips, in what looked like a flat expanse of beach. It was easy to get cut off as the rising tide sneaked in behind you, but they both knew the beach well. Michael was the pub landlord and for his sins was also a local councillor, knowing virtually everyone in the village, his little pub was a bit of a central hub. Rarely did anything happen in the village that he did not hear about. Many local clubs met there, in fact there were not enough nights in a week. The chess club, creative writing gathering, reading group, after choir eating place, and even more recently a knitting club. It enabled him to keep his ear to the ground and have an awareness of what was going on, good and only very occasionally bad, in the locality.

Dyfed and David had the central position searching the landward edge of the sand and the edge of the saltings. A fairly easy walk crossing the narrow mouths of many a small hillside stream emptying themselves pathetically onto the sand. In winter these could be raging torrents, gouging great channels in the sand and making their way directly into the sea.

The beach landscape was ever-changing with growing and receding saltings dependent on the winter weather.

Ceri and Tomos had drawn the short straw tonight, being the youngest on the team, they had been allocated the trickiest territory, right across the saltings up to the sea wall. Absolutely sure as dammit there would be wet feet before morning. They would have a hard time, certainly no time for banter. Dried out, ankle twisting ditches hid at every step, and some streams which had cut deep chasms needed jumping with accuracy and agility, not easy in your yellows and steel toe capped boots.

Dyfed's radio crackled to life, the comms were not good in the bay having both area masts well out of direct line, so all local communication needed to be through the Coastguard vehicles radio system which would relay messages, from the teams on the ground to the ops room at Holyhead. The radio was responding to one of the flank team members notifying of their arrival at the west end of the beach, with five on board, so again two teams of two, and one to stay with their truck to relay positions and progress to all concerned.

The police were not in contact other than by landline from their headquarters with the Coastguard ops room, so there was often a bit of delay in communications, but this was the norm. They all to some extent sounded like Daleks over the air, not that all the team members were even old enough to remember the Daleks of Dr Who fame.

Dyfed heard a familiar sound approaching from the south, a view of it obscured as yet, by the hill rising behind the beach, but recognising it as the local search and rescue helicopter which had been requested to assist. They had heat seeking equipment on board, but were still going to have a tough job covering the huge area. Normally they worked in grid squares as they did when searching over the sea.

Team progress along the sand was fairly hasty, he was aware of the torch lights to his left trailing behind, just because the terrain prevented his team-mates from making quick progress.

The order had been to make a hasty search initially, and then when the whole beach had been covered, to retrace their steps, but in what was termed a grid search formation, a little like what you would see police search teams doing following something like a suspected murder, maybe not quite a fingertip search but close enough. By the time they were ready to start that type of search, the second flank team would hopefully have arrived and be organised to join them, and probably be a little fresher. There may even be a couple more of his own team turning up, Gareth for instance worked nights until six am but had been known to turn up at a search for a couple of hours before collapsing into bed at lunchtime for a few hours kip before his night shift started again at six pm.

Dyfed loved the summer dawn, everything starting to wake up, bright rays of light appearing through the gaps in the forestry on the hillside which gradually crept further and further across the beach, like arrows of mottled light spearing towards the sand. He always thought on days like this, that he really ought to make the effort to get up early every summer's day, but somehow, it never seemed to happen, seven o'clock always seemed early enough, especially if he had not had a decent night's sleep, which was quite often the case these days.

Six am, his team-mates were making good progress, the pairs nearest the sea's edge were almost within touching distance of each other, being a fairly easy walk, keeping their eyes on the rapidly incoming tide, meaning they were mainly walking on an angle towards the shore. Every once in a while, the radios would squeak into life, team member just keeping tabs on each other. Soon the beach would be covered, and the call would go out to page the nearby inshore lifeboat to assist with the search. Later after the tide had gone out, a second search by the coastguard to cover the sand newly exposed, just in case anything had washed ashore, which had earlier been in the sea then spat out by the receding tide. The coastguard helicopter had by now been and gone with nothing found.

Life was returning to the beach with the dawn light, the cackle of gulls overhead, keeping a beady eye on the sea for mackerel and whitebait which was plentiful at this time of year, though in his opinion, gulls were now lazy bastards who preferred to hang around town and snatch sandwiches and ice creams out of the clutches of unsuspecting visitors. Some days it was like an episode of Hitchcock's 'The Birds', it was largely peoples own fault, they were too lazy in some cases to walk to a bin, so threw the fish and chip cartons on the floor, mind you the gulls were pretty clever and pulled out the rubbish from overfull overspilling bins. Seaside towns and villages had become easy pickings for the gulls. They could be quite vicious at times, particularly when the young hatched in the rooftop nests, and started early flying lessons. They had been known to land on peoples shoulders with a nasty peck of the ear or neck.

The cattle in the fields adjoining the sea wall were generally lying down in a group chewing their cud, not perturbed in the least by the activity on the beach.

The coastal path actually went along the sea wall at this point, so they were used to seeing the odd locals and visitors walking along the top of it, precariously passing each other in the widened sections so as to not fall down below into a swampy goo. On the seaward side the wall was almost 10-foot-high to its five foot on the landward side. A few years before, the local council had built a solid railed fence along the top of the wall to stop people falling off it. This was when he sea wall was included as part of the designated coastal path around the whole of the island. They still had the odd faller occasionally who had caught a foot in the fields wire fence which formed the inner edge, one person had gone head first into the field and broken their leg. Luckily nowadays most people carry a mobile phone. It hadn't been an easy job stretchering them to the road access, through the deep tractor ruts and cow muck that had built up over the winter.

Ceri and Tomos were now three quarters of the way along the beach, having got to slightly easier terrain, the flank team members had also covered the other end and were probably within three hundred metres of Ceri and Tomos. Once the teams met and were sure they had done a decent job, then normally they would just have a short break for refreshment, or a cigarette, which was the case with a couple of the team members, and they would restart the search from one end, and cover the whole area again. Everyone would this time be in a line closer together to start the grid search, this would cover the ground in far more detail and left no stone unturned. All the team members came together at six-thirty am, at the original rendezvous point, some were decidedly wet and dirty by now, after the odd trip and fall into the many holes in the saltings. Ceri was wet from the waist down, and didn't mind everyone hearing her complain loudly about it, though Aled would very much have preferred that she didn't swear quite so much. Another local team had now joined, so at least they had a few fresh people to give them a hand. Aled sent Ceri and Tomos home, secretly glad that Tomos had come in his own car, and could give Ceri a lift home to save soaking the seats in the coastguard truck. They may both be needed again later if the police decided to keep them searching the area.

Chapter Three

"COME HERE YOU LITTLE BUGGER," shouted Richard, as he strode purposefully along the woodland path, well-trodden now compared to years gone by, just because the local council had decided to assign it a footpath. It never used to be a designated footpath in his youth, in fact, it had simply been a route that locals would have walked to move between smallholdings in the area, he remembered as a boy how he had actually walked alongside his parents who silently followed a coffin, held high on the shoulders of a group of neighbours, bringing the body of someone's dearly departed from their home to the local church higher up the hill.

It was the way things were done locally then. He whistled again to no avail, what the hell had made him choose a Jack Russell terrier after his last faithful lab had died of old age, he didn't know, he often had his regrets as the dog ignored him yet again. There was no harm in him however, he was in the main a good dog, just a bit wilful.

It was easy to lose him in these woods, but he would always appear from somewhere with muddied snout, always investigating scents, poking around in some sort of hole in the ground. Today he was slower in coming back, but he always did in the end, so he

Community Killing

continued walking along the path, taking care that he didn't inadvertently trip over a surfacing tree root.

His attention had already been drawn that early morning to the activity going on down at the beach as the sun was rising, he had also heard the helicopter hovering nearby during the night. Some poor sod in trouble out at sea he imagined, when he had recognised the people as the local coastguard team members, he knew some of them. Dyfed who attended to his old car and somehow kept it mechanically sound, and David who taught at his grandsons' school and of course Aled who lived just at the other end of the woodland. They did a good job, called out all hours day or night. He admired people who actively volunteered to do these tasks.

He whistled again as he started to make his way slightly downhill, just aware all the time of the protruding roots. Margaret his wife always checked he had his mobile phone with him before he left the house, after an incident the summer before last, when he had fallen and badly twisted his ankle, and no one found him for ages as he had not taken his phone, or even thought to tell anyone which one of the hundreds of local forestry and woodland tracks he was walking. In fact, that time it was the little dog arriving home before him that alerted Margaret to anything being wrong, and eventually organise a search party from amongst the neighbours. It had taken him up to this last spring to really get over the ligament damage, and be able to enjoy his long walks again.

He could hear Scot yapping now at least and snarling, he must have come across something that didn't seem to please him very much , a fox maybe, it wasn't beyond him not to get caught up in a fight with a fox or the odd dog, that was the problem with these terriers, they thought they were bigger than any other dog. Scot came into view; he was certainly having a good bark at something, and in turn going forwards into the undergrowth then reversing in haste.

"It will just be a hedgehog," he thought to himself, he remembered seeing him do just that one evening in the garden when he has let him out for a last pee and a sniff around. "Come away you daft thing," he called- to no avail, not even a glance in his direction.

He realised in a few metres that Scot was just above the entrance of one of the two caves that were on the hillside, he had no real idea what their origins were, some said they were natural structures, others that they were part of a network of old mine workings from some ancient age or another, history had never been his strong point, he was very much more a science scholar. He used to play in them as a child, particularly if he was out with his mates on a rainy day. The one that Scot stood by now was the best cave, quite a drop down into the entrance hole, which was a bit of a squeeze for an adult but easy for a smaller child, and once in, it opened up so they could comfortably stand up. It had been a great adventure to come in here with some sneaked out candles and a couple of comics. They had even got a couple of old sacks to sit on. He smiled to himself as he reminisced.

He soon had the smile wiped off his face. Scot stepped back when Richard got to him, as if he had done his job, pointing out his find, Richard almost stumbled over in shock as he looked at his dogs discovery, immediately he turned away and vomited into the undergrowth, he never did have a strong stomach, and what he saw now just shocked him to the core, he stumbled back, grasping at the sapling next to him, it bent under his weight, he fell sideways and slithered a couple of feet down the slope, Scot was going berserk now in his excitement, more to do with Richard's behaviour than what he had found, he danced around Richard yapping and wagging his tail at this new game, with no inclination whatsoever of the enormity of what was going on. Richard recovered his feet, but half fell, half staggered a few feet away from the cave entrance, he grabbed at his jacket pocket, feeling for the weight of his mobile phone, he fumbled and got it out of his pocket, he punched the emergency number into it and spoke, he could barely breathe.

"What service do you require?" asked the voice.

"I don't know," rasped Richard

"Umm Police, maybe ambulance?"

"OK Sir," said the voice and proceeded to ask him to calm down, while they put him through to the local police call centre. They asked him where he was.

"Bloody hell, I don't know how to explain," he told them.

"I'm in the woods, above the bay, I haven't got a grid reference, I don't need one, I know my way around," he explained as best he could, and suggested the best access point for them, by coming down the Wern road and taking a right towards the farm of the same name, going off then along the footpath on the right, half-way down. Richard told them it was clearly signposted, and that they needed to cross the little bridge.

He put the phone down and tried to gather his wits about him, he clipped Scot onto his lead, the dog was quite strangely subdued by now. Richard didn't quite know how he felt, the initial rush of adrenaline had died down, allowing him to think a little more logically, however there was no way on earth he was going to be able to look in the cave entrance again, he had seen enough the first time. He could feel his heart hammering still in his chest, he walked towards a moss-covered boulder and sat himself down. They had told him to stay where he was, and they would call as they got to the woodland entrance, and that he should call back, so they could find him. They shouldn't take long. He was shaking, and still felt waves of nausea washing over him. He looked down through the trees and through a gap saw that the coastguard teams on the beach were being picked up by their vehicles and making off towards the eastern end of the beach, no doubt in order to return to the road and go up the hill back towards Allt Goch. Must have been a training exercise, bit early though he thought, not for a minute connecting what he had just found with their presence.

The sun was out now, the sky was blue, but he was chilled through to the bone. Scot whined, very likely bored with being made to sit still, Richard thought he might start making his way back the way he came, at least to the little bridge over the stream, there was a bungalow there, he knew the couple who lived there by sight, nice couple, they might spare him a tot of brandy, he could certainly do with it to calm his nerves and maybe warm him up inside. He had been told by a relative once that alcohol didn't really warm you up, that it was a false feeling, but at this very moment in time he honestly didn't care.

He pulled at Scot's lead, and went to turn away, just as a big crow flew down through the canopy and landed just by the cave entrance, a bloody hoody crow, that explained the couple he had seen earlier, damn them, carrion eating filth, he rushed forwards waving his arms, just enough to cause it to fly away, as he turned again, Scot was yapping, and wagging his tail excitedly, he could hear voices. Damn it he thought, he hadn't phoned Margaret, but no time for that now, the voices must be the police.

"Over here," he shouted, surprising himself with the weakness and hoarseness of his voice.

"Keep coming, I'm down this way." He half walked, half ran towards the voices, thinking, the sooner he directed them the sooner he could go home.

Three officers came towards him, and another in a suit which appeared to be two sizes too big for him, he introduced himself. "Detective Inspector Idris Huws," he said, "I'm assuming you are the first informant? Will you show me where she is please?"

"Over there," said Richard,

"I'm not going anywhere near the place, I've seen enough to have nightmares for years to come, terrible, terrible, who could have done such a thing, and here? Nothing bad ever happens here." He felt himself just getting a tad hysterical now, not really like him at all.

"Thank you, Sir, if you go with Sergeant Pritchard here, he will take you back to the road and drive you to the station." "The station? Why? Why do I need to go to the station, police station I assume, I need to go home and tell Margaret what's happened, she will be worried." The DI looked at him with a look on his face that Richard found difficult to read, but he wasn't sure he liked what he thought he saw. Was it sympathy or was it slightly accusatory.

"One of my officers has already gone down to your home and is with your wife now, she knows you are not hurt, but we will need to ask you some questions."

The third officer was now winding blue and white tape around the trees in the vicinity of the cave entrance.

"My God," thought Richard to himself, "this only happens to

people on television." He was worried about Margaret, she wasn't long home from hospital after a mild stroke. He followed the young sergeant, Scot, pulling ahead at the excitement of all the new people.

"Hey what about my dog?" asked Richard. "Oh, he will be fine with me, I love dogs," said the sergeant who Richard reckoned was about fifteen! They got younger and younger it seemed.

"I will run him back to your house when we have got you sorted at the station, don't worry it shouldn't take long, just a few questions, and fingerprints, ..." "What did you say? Fingerprints? What on earth for? I haven't done anything, I just phoned to tell the police what I had found.".

"It's just procedure Sir, don't worry about it."

Chapter Four

DYFED UNDID HIS LACES, kicked off his boots, and went into the kitchen. Hoover met him at the door with an old sock in his mouth, a present, Dyfed smiled and rubbed his head.

"Hi old boy, had your walk?"

"You talk to the dog before you talk to me," said Elin, but with a smile on her face.

"If you had texted to say you were on your way, I could have had breakfast ready for you."

"Sorry love, didn't think."

. . .

"What was it, false alarm, a hoax?" she asked getting some bits and pieces out of the fridge.

"No, I don't think so, not in this instance, something genuine I reckon, missing girl. They must have found her though as we were called off, though we haven't heard yet, with a friend probably, trouble at home because of boys apparently."

He sat down, glad to rest his feet for a minute, he would have a bite and get off to work, his lads were used to him by now, they were a good pair and would get on with their work till he arrived.

The Coastguard in general were rarely told by the police what the result of these types of searches were, and in fact the first they would hear would often be in the daily paper the next day, but in cases like this, mispers as they were referred to — missing persons, it was generally a family feud of one sort or another and nothing more was heard. He said goodbye to Elin, gave her a peck on the cheek and closed the door behind him, and off he went to do his normal working day.

Aled sat at the big pine table, coffee cup in hand, Jo his wife clearing away the breakfast dishes. He had a lot planned for today, the first job would be late to start now but would get done. He had another cut to make in the top fields, only five acres but a good number of silage bales would be made if he was lucky with the weather to add to the completed stack for the winter. He had fertilised this year, something he hadn't bothered with the last few years — the cost of the stuff was going up year by year, but he had cottoned on to the fact that he had a ready market for surplus bales amongst a couple of the local horse owning community, there were loads of horses and ponies around, he supposed having beach, forestry and miles of country lanes made it an attractive hobby.

. . .

The only thing he recognised was that some of these horses were kept, on owned or rented scraps of land which in this locality were not useful to the more serious local farmers, usually due to their steepness and the huge amount of rainwater run-off from the hill above, some were knee-deep in mud by the end of November. This year he reckoned he could balance out the cost of the fertilizer, if not even make a profit by creating a surplus. At twenty-five to thirty pounds a big bale, it wasn't bad money, though this year the wrap and the contractor had cost a fair bit.

He would get going with that in a minute after he had checked his post and e-mails, after all it was his accountancy work that helped him pay for the pleasure of living where, and how they did. It worked well, their lives had changed so much since moving full time to this glorious area of North Wales. He had spent most of his adult life to date, working for a large accountancy company on the edge of Manchester, and Jo had been a primary school teacher, they fell in love with the area on one of their many short breaks in the locality, and when they found Bryn Gwyn Bach advertised it was love at first sight. And the price had been very agreeable. It had needed a lot of work, it was registered by a Welsh preservation society, so they were limited to what they could do outside, but the inside was now beautifully renovated, and for a very old property, it was actually quite contemporary, and shocked many first-time visitors by its lightness and spaciousness compared to the image expected from the outside.

They had sold their Manchester suburbs house, where he had to admit he knew no one, not even his next- door neighbour. It had allowed them to buy Bryn Gwyn Bach, mortgage free and also money left over to do it up. They had managed to buy the cottage twenty- five years previously, and had been in the lucky position to be able to continue to live, and earn in Manchester, and do up the cottage whilst renting a small flat. In fact, he had moved there permanently way before Jo could give up her teaching position.

Jo did not miss her teaching job, unable to get a teaching position in a Welsh language stronghold, she had put all her efforts into helping Aled with the project of renovating the house and outbuildings, and helped him when needed with some paperwork. She had however, been invited with open arms into the community, and always had something on the go at the village hall.

They had a small flock of pedigree Dartmoor sheep, tough little buggers who coped easily with the relatively mild Anglesey winters. They were lucky that the land was sheltered, and dry in comparison with the general area, and they wintered out with very little supplementary feed. It was mainly a breeding herd, the lambs generally sold off to other smallholder hobby breeders. Jo never liked the idea of eating them, her own fault, giving the ewes names.

Today, he also had the first couple of clients bringing their accounts for the once over, before their end of October deadline for self-assessment tax returns. It was very different here from Manchester's organised paperwork. Many of his clients simply bought him carrier bags full of receipts and invoices, expecting him to do all the sorting and bookkeeping, and then working out their dues. It took hours, and they still whinged at the bill at the end of the day.

Jo had been out while Aled was still on the call-out and fed their small flock of hens and came back in with a bowl full of eggs, brown white and blue from some fancy breed she insisted on buying at the Royal Welsh winter fair last year. She used most of the eggs herself, baking and cooking but loved to be able to hand out half a dozen when friends visited.

"What's going on in the woods today?" she asked, seems to be loads of voices coming from there".

"Haven't a clue," answered Aled barely turning his head from the computer screen in front of him.

"I think I will take a stroll and have a look," said Jo.

"OK, I will just see what's on here then I will get the mower out and get cutting, I should be finished for a late lunch then, if I get on with it now," he answered

After a quick check through e-mails, and deciding there was nothing urgent, Aled closed down the computer and changed into his work boots, stuck his favourite check shirt over his T-shirt and walked over to the shed where the tractor was kept. The new shed was really the only addition to the place since they had moved in. A modern agricultural building where lived the tractor and the few implements he had gathered together, the mower, topper, harrows, roller and fertilizer spinner, all bought second hand at local farm auctions. He had a few pens in here too, for the ewes for when they lambed. They didn't ever plan the lambing until march, unlike the Christmas lambs he often saw hereabouts. He loathed to see two and three-day old lambs huddling and shivering, in the awful weather that December to February could throw at them. He had built the shed just for night-time convenience close to the house, they had learnt their lesson the second year they were there, when they lost more than their fair share to a local fox population from lambing the flock outdoors.

He had been lucky to source his tractor, a not too huge Massey Ferguson, four-wheel drive model, as rare as hens' teeth apparently, front loader and everything for handling the bales through the winter. He delivered the odd bale locally, as most of the local horse owners had no means of transporting or moving them into place, and only wanted one at a time.

He heaved the diesel can onto the tractor bonnet, then using the funnel he filled its tank. Hopping up the step into the cab. He turned on the radio above his head, mind you he thought to himself he would do better to concentrate on what he was doing than listening to a debate on Radio Four.

Jo walked to the end of their drive, more a track really. She loved it, still retaining a thick strip of grass in the middle along its length, mind you some of their more townie visitors didn't appreciate it with their low-slung cars, some even parked them at the entrance and walked to the farm, easily a half mile walk. Not always best pleased, dependent on their choice of shoes, they had been warned, but most forgot about their discomfort when they entered what they saw as a slightly ruinous old cottage, to see the beautifully designed Scandi style interior. Spacious and light, the huge inglenook filling one end, and a full height ceiling giving a totally deceiving image to what most people expected. The track ended at a kissing gate on their boundary and continued then as a pathway through unkempt old woodland. In fact, the fields next door were involved in some family dispute or another over ownership and access, and had not been grazed for as far as she knew, over twenty years, they were now liberally dotted with over ten-year-old self- sown saplings. At this time of year, the path was barely used, being so overgrown, only the dedicated local walkers pushing their way through the long grass bracken and nettles. Once through the overgrown field which actually extended to her right, over the shoulder of the hill, you entered a slightly denser area of woodland, which had a clear path through to the little hamlet beyond. Her favourite time of year was the spring, which locally gave the woods their name of Bluebell woods. There was a huge acreage of wild unclaimed land in the immediate area, probably two to three hundred acres of wilderness to a certain degree in all. None of it currently farmed, though some effort was being made at the top of the hill to reclaim an old farmstead, where the long-time residents had died, and the property had been left to someone outside the area. Good luck to them, thought Jo, it would take a pretty penny to get it workable and productive again. She could hear voices again now but couldn't hear well enough to make out what was going on, but as she was about to drop down a little slope to cross a small stream, she was stopped in her tracks, by firstly some blue and white coloured tape across the path and then the back of a police officer.

"What's going on?" she asked. The young policeman had obviously had his mind elsewhere and not heard her approach, as he tried to disguise his surprise and blocked her path.

"I'm sorry madam, I can't allow you to continue along this path today, we have some work going on here and the footpath is blocked until further notice."

"Oh, I live just across the field in the farm at the end of the track, I was alerted by voices and wondered if maybe someone was lost, what's happened?"

. . .

"I'm sorry I'm not at liberty to say, and in fact will have to ask you to return the way you came and leave the area."

"But ....."

"I'm sorry Madam, I don't make the rules," he was still polite but it was pretty obvious from his manner that he totally meant what he said, there was no going for a nosey for her. Just as she was about to turn away, she caught a glimpse of another person about a hundred metres ahead, in a white coverall head to toe. Obviously, something not so nice had happened. She turned back and retraced her steps to the farm. It was pointless either ringing or texting Aled, he wouldn't hear above the sound of the machinery, she would have to walk to the top field to tell him. She noticed as she emerged in a clearing that there was a helicopter approaching from the southeasterly direction, over the crest of the hill at the other end of the beach, and making its way in her direction, she recognised it as a police helicopter from the local force as opposed to the search and rescue helicopter that had been about in the early hours. Aled saw the helicopter too, but paid it no heed as he set off on the next row of sward to be cut.

Chapter Five

RICHARD DRANK the last dregs of the coffee he had been given by the young officer. His hands had really only just stopped shaking from the shock of the find that morning. He knew Margaret had arrived at the station, as he had heard her voice, but as yet he had not been allowed to see her. He had only been allowed to have a pee, after explaining that his old bladder wasn't as reliable as it had been, before the joys of the old water tablets that were prescribed to him, they were a total pain, and dictated totally his movements for a few hours through the morning, until their effect had worn off, but they were doing their job, he supposed alongside the rest of the concoction that he took for his dodgy ticker.

The door opened, and the same young officer walked in.

"You are free to leave Sir, but we may well need to talk to you again at some point in our enquiries."

"But you haven't asked me anything?" exclaimed Richard.

"No, it's OK Sir, we have verified your whereabouts this morning through a couple of witnesses, so you are free to go."

"Thank God for that, I could do with a sit down in my own chair, with a tot of whisky in my hand."

"I'm sure Sir, thank you for your time this morning, but you have to understand we have to dot the I's and all that."

Margaret was by the front desk when he left the room, she stepped forwards and squeezed his hand.

"Come on love, let's get you in the car and home, you have had a terrible time by the sound of it."

Once in the car, Richard belted up in the passenger side, Margaret, did most of the driving these days, it had become the norm since he had badly injured his leg, though there had been a slight question about her still doing so, after the stroke. It was however deemed so mild, her doctor allowed her to continue. Richard put his head in his hands and rubbed his eyes.

"I'm speechless," he said. "I have no words for what I have seen this morning, and I doubt very much whether I will ever get the vision out of my minds-eye ever again, it makes me sick to the stomach to think about it, the poor love. Who the hell around here would do such a thing to another human being?"

"Forget it now for a bit Love, let's just get you in the house, though whether we can get down our road I don't know, the place was crawling with police cars and vans, parked everywhere when I drove up the hill. They had to park on the road and walk down the track to get to the entrance of the woods, and the top of the track is all taped off with policemen standing guard there. It must be those scenes of crime people like you see on TV because a few of them were in overalls with gloves and face masks on."

Richard sat in silence for the remainder of the short drive home, he felt that if he said or thought too much, he would burst into tears, like a small hysterical child. Sure enough as they came to the junction at the top of their road in the village, there was a police car parked. They stopped, and after a brief chat, Margaret was allowed to drive on towards home.

"I had to get the postman to vouch for you being at home this morning, and Peter and Diane told them they had seen you pass their house and turn into the woods at whatever time they saw you, they must have been happy with that information". "Hmm" answered Richard. "Still managed to make me feel like a criminal when in fact I was a sort of victim to have had to see what I did."

He slammed the car door, and went in through the back door, Scot met him happily wagging his tail.

"Hey old boy, come on let's go through and sit down, you have seen horrors today as well haven't you? If only dogs could talk." He slumped into his chair, and breathed a sigh of relief at being home, but he noticed his hands still had a tremor, Margaret came back in the room and passed him a welcome glass of malt.

The phone rang in the kitchen, he heard Margaret answer it, then obviously close the door so as not to disturb him, or else prevent him from hearing the conversation. She needn't have worried, along with his other aches and pains, his hearing wasn't the best now either. Margaret re entered the room.

"That was Jo, Aled's wife, she wanted to know what the police were doing in the woods, and thought maybe we would have seen or heard something at this end. Aled was trying to finish the top fields and asked her to phone. I told her what you said you found, I hope I haven't done wrong, she is horrified and I think a bit scared, she has gone back to tell Aled". "Ah well, no doubt everyone will know something soon anyway, once the newspaper reporters get hold of this sort of thing, they will be here in their droves", he stopped at this point as if this fact had only just entered his head. "Oh, for God's sake if anyone comes nosing around here asking questions tell them I have nothing to say to them". He finished off his glass of whisky and shouted, "another". His head fell back, and he closed his eyes, trying hard, but failing to obliterate the terrible visions playing out inside his eyelids, like the worst ever horror film.

Aled could see Jo running up between the rows of cut grass. Something must be up he thought, his Joanne didn't usually run anywhere for anybody, being slightly cuddly as she liked to describe herself, she was no cross-country runner as her bright red face proved when she reached him. He stopped the engine as she bent down hands on knees catching her breath. "There's been a murder," she blurted out. "In our wood's, a young woman, according to Margaret." Jo gasped to draw in her breath.

"Worst of all, it was Richard who found her, when walking the dog early this morning, he has only just come home from the police station in Bangor now." She gulped noisily again as Aled said,

"Do we know who she is?" A horrible thought had immediately put two and two together in his head, the young girl they had been searching for earlier, the search had been called off with no explanation from the police, much as happened normally. His team had all gone home and about their daily business, and the poor girl had been found by Richard no more than a field away from the farm. "No, I don't think Margaret or Richard knew that."

"That's terrible, come on I will come down to the house with you, could do with a cuppa, I will phone Richard myself and see what's going on, but murder? Here? That's too much to imagine. Who the hell would be capable of doing something like that, nothing ever happens here apart from a petty burglary, a chainsaw or strimmer from an unlocked shed? Come on."

His mobile rang, it was Michael from the pub in the village, one of his buddies from the Coastguard team, like himself, Michael would have gone home from the search this morning straight back to whatever needed doing at the pub, or more likely, attending some meeting or another at the local council offices in the nearest town. He was tempted to ignore the call, in favour of looking after Jo who was clearly upset.

"Hi," he said.

"Yes, I've just heard, who told you about it?" He listened nodding his head at whatever was being said.

"Right OK, will let you know if I hear any more, bye."

"I can't believe this is happening so close to us here, we moved from Manchester, to get away from stuff like this," said a tearful Jo. Aled placed his arm loosely over Jo's shoulder as they set off down the field towards the cottage.

Chapter Six

DYFED PICKED up his mobile phone from the work bench, he glanced at the screen, it was Aled.

"Hi, have you heard anything from this morning's job yet?" Before Aled could say anything.

"No mate, not as such, but a young girl's body has been found in the woods, not too far away from me here, mutilated apparently, but I'm not wanting to make assumptions, but likely it's the young girl we were looking for."

"Oh shit," said Dyfed, then turned to the entrance of the back office so the lads couldn't hear him.

"Do you mean she has been murdered? Here in Allt Goch?"

"I'm not saying that," said Aled,

"I'm just telling you what I've heard, the police are there now, no doubt we will all hear something soon on the news or something, the area is all taped off. Jo went over there to see what all the voices were and got sent away with a flea in the ear. I will let you know if I find anything more. Old Richard down the hill found her, or rather his dog did, dead upset he is too, obviously, let me know if you hear anything."

Dyfed disconnected the call, then just as quickly, dialled Elin's mobile number and repeated what he had been told. She was speechless and told Dyfed she would let him know if she heard something, but that would be unlikely.

"That's not why I'm telling you," he said.

"If this is a murder then whoever has done it is still out there, come straight here from work and I will close up early and go home at the same time as you, I don't want you to be alone."

Word soon got out amongst the local residents; the phone lines were hot with people trying to get any news. Jungle drums. It was a big story in the area, nothing like this ever happened in this small corner of Wales, well not since a henpecked husband clobbered his wife with an iron, killed her and buried her in the sands of Red Wharf Bay. That was way back in 1945 though. A long time ago now. The conclusion at this time had already been decided hereabouts that it was the young missing girl Sarah Jones.

Ceri Thomas picked up her mobile, it was John her Coastguard colleague.

"Fucking hell," she said after a couple of seconds listening.

"Remind me never to get a bloody dog, it's always dog walkers that find this sort of thing, isn't it", she said. "Poor girl, is it definitely her?"

She stayed on the phone only another second, and couldn't switch it off fast enough to phone Tomos, who had also been on the search job with her.

He responded with silence, stunned silence.

"Where did John hear this?"

"Everyone seems to know," she answered. "The old boy that lives at the bottom of the hill the other end of the forest, found the body this morning when he was out walking his dog", she spoke as if it was the most exciting thing that had ever happened to her.

"Hmm, probably while we were still out on the beach looking for her. No wonder we were stood down with no real explanation, not that that in itself was unusual."

Chapter Seven

DI HUWS HAD ALWAYS, and would always, hate the building in the local hospital that housed the morgue and the autopsy room. His very first attendance at a post-mortem examination had been as a young constable, and that was a local sudden death with what was thought then to be suspicious circumstances. He had worked very hard to fight back the nausea, and failed dismally to his embarrassment. It was always more the smell. A lingering, cloying, thick sort of smell that you couldn't get out of your nostrils for hours after it was all done and dusted. A young colleague of his at the time, had told him he needed to plug his nostrils with Vicks inhaler cream, just before he went into the room, which he duly did. Oh yes, certainly it helped block out the smell, but by god, his eyes ran so much that he couldn't see what was going on, he spent the time with a hanky wiping his eyes and denying that he was weeping at the procedure in front of him. He hadn't done that again in a hurry. He hadn't been allowed to forget it either, his mates at the time nick naming him Vick, thankfully it didn't follow him to his next station. Now he tended to just be a little heavy-handed with a spray bottle of aftershave, he kept in his car for these occasions. Over time he had hardened a little to the procedure. Some autopsies however still had the power to shock him.

The Pathologist, was just putting on his overalls and gloves, as Idris Huws arrived, much as a surgeon would do in a theatre with a live person to work on. The body was laid in front of a glass screened area still covered with a sheet. Thankfully, nowadays he was separated by the screen, in a totally separated glass-walled room with full view, and a speaker to communicate, state of the art apparently, being the only large hospital facility for many miles, all autopsies in the area were done here.

Earlier that day he had escorted the young girls' distraught parents to view and identify the body, not an easy task considering the attack that had taken place on her body, her face was thankfully intact but her neck had to be very carefully hidden from their view. She had been identified as 15-year-old Sarah Jones. He never enjoyed that part, delivering the agony message to already distraught people must in fact be one of the worst aspects of the job. He would never forget the wails of distress that emanated from within these people, they were broken to the core. He hated it.

Now, the task of finding the cause of death, would start in detail. Very little helpful evidence having being found at the scene, although the scenes of crime team would still be working there, that would continue for a while yet, all the evidence gathering would take a while, though he knew full well that likely the scene had already been contaminated by the old man and his dog. That he knew, couldn't have been helped. It was hoped that more information would become apparent during the postmortem. Idris Huws certainly hoped so, they needed to get this particular perpetrator behind bars as soon as humanely possible, considering how viciously they had attacked this poor girl's body. Idris had seen the aftermath of a few murders over the years, but had to admit to himself, this was the worst one to date.

It had become clear from talking to the parents, that the row they had was a heated one, and Sarah had walked out. Her mother had wanted to go after her, but Steven Jones her father had insisted that Sarah would not go far and would be back sulking soon enough, how wrong he had been. Mrs Jones was now totally distraught that the last communication she had with her daughter, had been bitter words between them, accusatory words, horrible words that she would have done anything to be able to take back.

In cases like this, though, thankfully, he had not had to deal with many murders in his small quiet patch of Wales, he found that very often tragedies of this kind, more often than not broke up what had always been close families, the grief, the pain, leading to accusations, and blame, and very often at the end of the line, the divorce courts.

Rowlands the pathologist drew back the sheet, he had a tendency to drama, and Huws would swear that Rowlands held his breath a bit, Idris on the other hand was reluctant to take in the scene in front of him. But it was unavoidable, both men stood silently gazing down for long moments. What Idris saw was a repeat of the nightmare scene that had faced him in the forest. The young victim was laid on her back, her hair tidily pulled back behind her, but streaked with mud, her throat was gaping open with a wound so brutal that he imagined that neither of them had seen its like before. This was no knife wound, her throat structures were described slowly and calmly by Rowlands. Her trachea and oesophagus, jugular veins and carotid arteries had been torn, she would have bled out very quickly, however he wasn't sure at this point whether this would have been the first wound, inflicted on this poor girl. He added that he hoped it was, as the alternative didn't bear thinking about. Her abdomen was open and exposed, from her sternum, virtually to her pubic area, a whole mess, as far as Huws could see, of guts torn and trailing.

Rowlands was by now working slowly and silently and minutes seemed to pass before he spoke again. Everything he said was recorded by the speaker over the table, not just for the purpose of the viewers behind the glass door being able to hear, but everything was kept on record. It would obviously as always, be evidence one day in court.

"DI, would you please come through for a few moments, you need to see this at closer quarters I'm afraid. Jane here will get you some PPE." Pausing now, and turning his back to the table, as if relieving himself of the sight in front of him for a few seconds respite. His eyes were shut.

Within a minute Huws was silently looking at the absolute total mess in front of him, the only part of the poor girl that was unmarked, was indeed her face and lower legs. The rest of her was either torn, disembowelled or deeply lacerated. The injuries were deep and dirty, filled with debris, soil and gravel from where she was found.

"I hope her neck wound was the first she suffered," said Rowlands. "Believe me, in all my years of pathology, this is like nothing I've ever seen before, totally barbaric and inhumane. Carried out I would say by someone in an utter frenzy." Silence, neither of them knew quite what to say or do for the moment, stunned. Rowlands had put down his instruments and was busying himself trying to tidy up the scene in front of him. Normally the bodily organs would have been weighed and replaced, however there were none to weigh, her liver, spleen and stomach had gone. Her chest cavity had not been penetrated, but any remaining intestines were carefully replaced back in the abdominal cavity, and Rowlands placed a thin layer of plastic over her before replacing a clean sheet over the body. Huws believed, at that moment in time, that the image would forever be etched in his brain, and would surely be the visions of future nightmares.

He followed Rowlands out of the room, after he and Jane had slid the poor girl's body into one of the many fridges in the adjoining room. What tales could that girls spirit tell. He sat down in Rowlands office; Rowlands had his head in his hands, not a word passed his lips for what seemed many minutes.

He opened a drawer in his desk, bought out a bottle of Whisky and three glasses. One each for himself and Huws, and one for his assistant Jane, who had stayed behind to wash down the autopsy area. She would join them shortly.

"Sorry, I can't drink on duty," said Huws looking longingly at the glass of brandy being poured".

"Take it," said Rowlands, we all need it. He didn't resist for long. He held it in his hands for barely a few seconds, then downed it all in one, followed by a hasty retreat to the nearby lavatory, his hand tightly clasped over his mouth.

"That was a waste of bloody good whisky," muttered Rowlands as Huws returned to his seat, mopping his sweaty brow with his hanky. His face a horrible shade of pasty grey Another glass was waiting for him on the desk. "Keep that one down, it's good stuff, too good to waste."

Jane joined them, having removed her coveralls and took a chair in the corner. She had clearly been crying. She was normally a tough nut, having done this job almost from leaving school, she had seen some sad sights, but this was totally beyond anything that had gone before. The fact that her long-time colleague had simply gone to the office and sat down, was telling. Normally he would have helped with the clean-up, whistling while he worked, making the odd dry joke, as was per usual amongst people who worked amongst the dead, day in day out, never at the expense of the deceased, or at least very rarely, just general banter, so that they went home after having enjoyed a bit of a laugh. People outside of these occupations rarely understood it, thinking them hard and a tad offensive. It was between the two of them, and they always took care that the observation room had been vacated.

Chapter Eight

THE MEETING WAS CALLED for 8am, DI Huws taking charge. He had to admit to being just a tad apprehensive, this was more than likely the biggest job of his career. He would not call the area a backwater, but other than the nagging wife case, the Nettletons, before his time and the odd burglary, he was lucky to cover a relatively peaceful part of this corner of Wales. It would more than likely be his last big job before his retirement in a couple of years' time too.

Anyway, he needed to get his team briefed, and the post-mortem photos that he had in the A4 envelope would no doubt be pinned onto the wall, in the room which had been requisitioned in the local community centre as their base during the case, the local police station just did not have a big enough room. Huws also preferred to work amongst the community where the incident happened, it often gleaned more information.

His officers this time, however work hardened, would be shocked to see the pictures. He passed the brown envelope to his detective sergeant, he pulled them out all together then slowly walked to the wall without looking at the pictures. He singled the first one out and tucked the others under his arm as he reached up for the pins. This bought the photo right to his eyeline, Huws was convinced he heard a gasp as he dropped the main pile on the floor and just pinned the first onto the wall.

"Come on now Howard, get on with it lad," said Huws, knowing the poor man was clearly shocked.

The photos were pinned up one by one in all their gruesome horror and one by one the team stopped talking as their eyes fell on the photos. Howard stood dumbstruck a couple of steps back from the wall. Huws let them have a minute to absorb what they were seeing. He felt for them, some were still relatively young, certainly they would not have seen anything like this before. He had gone home and tightly hugged his teenage daughter last night, much to her surprise, they had never been a family that hugged each other for no particular reason, which seemed to be the norm nowadays, in fact his daughter seemed to think that he and his wife were the worst parents ever, at the moment, but that was just adolescence, he was a little the same at the same age.

"Right, I think we can all see what we have here, it's unbelievable what some of us had to witness yesterday, and we need to get to the bottom of this as quickly as is humanly possible. Whoever is out there capable of doing this is extremely dangerous and needs to be caught, before this can happen again, so come on, where do we start."

"Fingerprints?" said a young PC drafted in to do some basic leg work on the case, as were a few others.

"There were no fingerprints," said Huws. "No obvious footprints at the scene either, they are still looking. Down at the scene area was just loose soil and grit and very disturbed but so far not a shoe print or any other trace of anyone having walked down there that day, other than the old guy who found her." He paused, not convinced the team were totally listening, they were still staring at the photos. "Cause of death can not be exact as yet, other than the actual injuries would have caused her to bleed out very quickly, the hope in reality is that the first attack was maybe from behind to the neck, so that she may even have been dead before her disembowelment, I can only hope. This was clearly a frenzied attack by some nutcase who, once he started, totally lost it. He paused for effect, to allow the full enormity of what they were dealing with to sink in. Her liver and spleen have been removed, and they have not been found as yet, there is now a fingertip search going on as we speak, but clearly, it's difficult taking into account the wooded, extremely hilly terrain.

"There was also no physical evidence of sexual assault, in fact she was fully clothed from the waist down. As you can see, she was eviscerated, the contents of her abdomen were not surgically removed but torn out, her trousers and panties were still on. Forensics are still doing further tests, they will obviously check for semen internally and externally as per usual, but so far, no fibres, hairs or any evidence has been found which could have been deposited by the killer, her shirt has been ripped to shreds. Whoever has done this has certainly covered their tracks. There is an inkling in the higher echelons that it could be some sort of act of black magic, but there is nothing solid to confirm that either at this point in time. I certainly hope to God, that does not prove to be the case."

"Sir, do we have any idea regarding the weapon?" Asked a young **WPC** who was busy taking notes.

"No, we don't. As I have said already, none of the wounds were incised, they were torn, lacerated I think was the term used, whatever instrument has been used, at the moment, I just cannot imagine." He imagined that she just had not processed in her young brain what she was hearing and saying, in fact he didn't think he had assimilated it yet himself.

"We need to get out there now and ask some questions, house to house, every single house in the area before whatever nut job has done this gets away, though more than likely they have legged it anyway. Remember, holiday cottage changeover day is upon us soon, so if a bunch of you can concentrate on any addresses we have locally and cover them first, that might help, if someone has seen or heard anything strange or someone acting suspiciously. There are a couple of cottage agents around locally, maybe Beaumaris or Menai Bridge, see if they can help you with a list of addresses, and maybe even names of anyone who may have been on a short break for a few days, or any properties which have been vacated early. Rest of you get in amongst the locals, it will be everywhere by now anyway, you know what the jungle drums are like hereabouts."

He looked around the room, normally people would be bustling about now getting on with various tasks or looking at any tiny lead to follow. Today there was a sombre silence, stunned, he imagined.

"Go on then, get on with it."

Chairs scraped the floor as people got up, papers shuffling, laptops shut down, and some switched on by others, searching no doubt for contact numbers of various parties, a couple pausing to look closer at the photos as they passed.

"Howard, you get down to the forest see if SOCO have come up with anything new."

"Yes Sir."

Policing had changed since Huws started, as a young cadet, he was married to the job, hence his late marriage and entry into the world of fatherhood. He had been mentored through the ranks, and because he was single, had not been granted a police house, but had lived in a variety of digs in whichever village he had been posted to, and they were quite a few. Mainly rural stations. Most villages having a police house and a local bobby on the beat who knew his patch, and every single person on it good and bad. Most jobs had been petty burglaries, a few speeding fines, always a local willing to grass on others, to seek favour for whatever wrong doing they may have been involved in themselves. His birth era had been at the very end of the hippy era, there were loads of them dotted around this area having moved into semi-derelict cottages on hillsides that the locals looked at in disdain, in favour of their seventies housing estates, many built by local cowboy builders cashing in on the sixties baby boom and the need for housing. Most of these hippies were mature people now, carving a living for themselves in a whole variety of ways. Some had lost their homes in the early to mid-seventies to language nationalists who set incendiary bombs off in their houses, particularly if they thought they were holiday homes in the effort to keep the area welsh. Welsh was, and still was the local language despite their claims it would die out, the primary schools were Welsh and most incomers integrated well, and made great efforts to learn the lingo. Most of the activists were now also mature in age and attitude. Policing was very much at local level with larger town stations and then the HQ for the area in Caernarfon.

Now the policing was very much more distant, he now didn't know some of his police colleagues further afield, times had certainly changed. Some of the team sent here now for this job, he was not familiar with, but no doubt that would change over the next few days. Hopefully not weeks or months.

Chapter Nine

MIKE AND STEVE paddled quietly around the headland. It was a glorious day, sun shining in the azure sky and just the hint of a breeze, barely tangible. An ideal day for it. They had each driven with their wives down to Penmon point, and been dropped off with their kayaks, and whilst the ladies had gone for a coffee in the old white cottage which now served as a café, they got their togs on ready to launch. Wet suits and lightweight anorak and buoyancy aid on, and mobiles in their waterproof pouches. Plans for the day had been made. A paddle around the headland to Llanddona Bay where their cars and respective wives would be waiting for them, no doubt after a bit of retail therapy in Beaumaris on the way through. They both enjoyed their jaunts on their sit on kayaks, preferring them these days to the sit in variety they once had, capsizing and trying to get out now at their ages was not as easy as it used to be, they used to fish for mackerel in the past and virtually fill their kayak to almost sinking point with fish. Those days were long gone. Now in their early seventies just being able to get from A to B safely without mishap was an achievement.

The view from the perspective of the sea around this headland was always a pleasure, shingle beaches at Penmon giving way to steeper cliffs and rock shelves, old quarry workings and narrow rock clefts, before giving way to the expanse of golden sands of Llanddona beach, which just blended onwards at its western end into the popular Red Wharf Bay.

There was a fair depth of water under them at the base of the cliffs but so clear and blue was it today sparkling in the sunlight, necessitating the use of sunglasses against the glare. Steve wished he had used some sunscreen, being fair he would no more than likely look like a lobster later on that evening. He had refused the offer of some from Kate when they parked, however, he knew full well that she was always annoyingly right, and she reminded him of that at every opportunity.

Getting around the first corner from the steep shingle beach at Penmon itself was the only particularly challenging part of the paddle, where the swell could still be a leftover from the tide racing through the Sound between the mainland and Ynys Seiriol, but once they had slipped around the corner it would be a fairly leisurely paddle. They passed the huge fish farm, a blot from the sea but thankfully well hidden from the landward side, here the coastal path diverted well away from it. Many locals did not even know it was there. On past Shore house — a lonely cottage just set back off the edge. Mike had always wondered about its history, it was a fair way down from the track off the lane at Caim too, he presumed it was a holiday cottage now like many others in the area.

The paddle from Shore house to their first break point at White beach was a fair distance for two old boys, but there was no rush at all on a day like this, so onwards they went, both enjoying the calm, other than the squawking gulls above them and the odd seal popping bottling above the surface, keeping a beady eye on their territory invaders.

White beach, or Traeth Gwyn to give it its local name, was a beautiful hidden shingle cove, popular with local fishermen for its seasonal Mackerel, Whitebait and Bass, but also the curse of the amateur fisherman who chose to cast off his line from atop the rocky promontories. Tackle would be lost numerous times from getting caught on the jagged rocks down in the depths, it was not rare either for a cheeky seal to steal a hooked fish off the line before it could be hauled in. The best results were often achieved at low tide. The small bay had once housed a quarry and jetty, blown up in the seventies. The remains of an old water tank were still at the top, where the road to the headland ended, leading onto Fedw Fawr, an area of local natural beauty.

Most tourists to the area completely missed out on White beach, it was not waymarked at the top of the road and being single track for a fair distance, many town dwellers were simply scared of venturing down the road, for fear of needing to reverse, which many of them seemed totally incapable of doing.

They reached the shore and slightly struggled to pull both kayaks up the shingle slope, small rocks and rounded boulders slithering and sliding under their feet, making progress difficult. The beach was empty. Ten minutes were spent stretching stiffening legs, but mainly savouring the silence. For whatever reason there weren't even many birds about today this far around the headland, most likely they hung around the lighthouse area and the mouth of the Menai Strait.

After a breather, the kayaks were noisily slid down the shingle bank again, both men ankle deep before carefully getting back onto their transport. Soon they were beyond Fedw Fawr, heading now towards the next stretch of shingle which was the area known as Tan Dinas quarry, another one long abandoned. A few cottages were above on the headland, accessed by a track that had suffered a landslip and become impassable a few years before, and the hamlet of Pentre Llwyn which had housed a few quarry workers, as had many of the cottages in the village of Llanddona up atop the hill.

Neither had ever paddled into this Bay.

"Shall we pull in here and have a look around?" said Mike.

"Yes, go on then, we have time, the girls won't be back for another hour at least and it's a nice day", answered Steve. It was a rocky shore similar to White beach, large pebbles rounded off by centuries of hammering by westerly gales. The slope up this beach however was far steeper than White beach, creating difficulties for by now, increasingly fatigued legs, as they made their way up the stone ridges. They took care to pull their kayaks well out of the water, **in case** they simply slid back into the sea. It had been known to happen to them before. Many stones here were quite unique, some had holes right through and the occasional fossil to be found.

They made their way closer to the cliff face. Quarry work ended many years ago, and there were remains of just a couple of buildings. There was the usual evidence however of human spoil, the ring of stones created as a firewall for a makeshift barbecue, remnants of charred sticks and what Mike particularly hated, rusting empty beer cans.

"Why the hell don't people just take out what they bring in," he muttered.

"Sheer laziness and lack of respect for the environment probably," answered Steve. "It doesn't half stink around here though, I shan't be staying long, must be a dead sheep around somewhere."

"Hmm," said Mike.

"Or a seal."

Whether it was because it was unfamiliar territory, or because of the stench they decided to move on.

"Hang on for a minute," said Mike.

"I need a pee first." Off he disappeared to the left of the big roofless brick shed towards the lee of the cliff, probably a dynamite store or similar when the quarry was productive.

"Jesus Christ Almighty," shouted Mike as he reappeared,

"There is a rotting human corpse here, behind the shed, not much left of it, bones picked dry by carrion I should think, we need to phone the police."

"Bloody hell, are you sure? Is it not maybe the remains of a seal or porpoise that you have seen?" said Steve.

"I've never seen a seal wearing trainers, have you? Have you still got that App you showed me on your phone, to be able to give the police a grid reference?"

Chapter Ten

"RIGHT LADS, it's Explorer 263 and grid reference 583 821," said D I Huws. This declaration made him sound smarter, however, it was just passing on information passed to him by a young constable who had simply been given to him by the first informants on scene.

"Any of you lads or ladies' experts in map reading? I'm just going to pass the details on to the Coastguard Ops room in Holyhead, but we need to see where we can get to the scene by the easiest and nearest access point, a decomposed body has been found on a beach somewhere around Penmon. We need to close it off and stop any public getting there."

"That should not be a problem Sir," said a voice from the back of the room, Constable Pete Smith, a keen hill walker was already on to it on his computer. "There is very little chance we will get there other than on foot, the nearest cottage by track is Bodola and from then on its just marked as a path, not even really a public one. More than likely just an old quarryman's path, so it may well be impassable, there has also been a landslide between the lane and Bodola track, so we will need to walk in, unless we can be taken by sea?"

Two hours later, after a lot of organising, Huws was overseeing

Community Killing

the RNLI crew and Coastguard volunteers bagging the deceased, they had to organise two trips from Beaumaris to bring SOCO to the scene. All relevant photos had been taken, and it seemed a bit daft to keep the scene as found for any longer than needed today, they could get on with the post-mortem, and he could get a team here first thing in the morning, to look around for any other evidence. He was quite certain that there had not been anyone at the scene or it would most certainly have been reported . Being off the beaten track and barely accessible he was quite happy in himself to release the body, and the two gents who had found it. Steve and Mike were to be taken back to Beaumaris in the lifeboat, the crew carefully secured the men's Kayaks across the stern. They both sat motorbike style behind the helmsman, certainly a quicker way back. It would have been quite exhilarating had it just been for any other reason.

The boat trailer was already in the water, waiting to re-house the boat, masses of people watching and taking photos, totally oblivious to what had been developing, not two miles away or so as the crow flies. Marian and Kate were already there, Steve having phoned them from the beach, without telling them the full story but emphasising that they were both just fine.

The scenes of crime officers had not been very long deciding that there was very little to be found at the location of the body, no evidence of anyone else having been involved, no footprints to be seen or any tyre tracks anywhere near the top of the quarry, other than tractor tracks belonging to the neighbouring landowner, he had no cause whatsoever to make his way down the track to the quarry as it wasn't part of his tenancy. Within a few hours the scene looked as if no one had set foot there ever.

Huws walked up the slope from the beach, blowing, he couldn't actually walk and talk at the same time with the SOC officer who accompanied him. He made a note to make more effort with his level of fitness or at least lay off the pies and pastries which were always an easy to grab snack during the day. He had taken off his waterproof jacket on the ascent, sweat was pearling on his forehead. He wiped at it with a handkerchief out of his trouser pocket.

His car was parked car at the nearest point to the path, a pull in on a bend near the base of an old hill fort, apparently occupied prior to the Roman invasion. On a rare day off, he had walked to its flat top with the dog, you could see right enough why this would have been chosen for its all-around view. As far as the Isle of Man on a haze free day. Towards the west of the island, and clear views towards the mainland of Gwynedd, fantastic views of the Snowdonia hills. This slight variation to the planned route had been pointed out to them by a local who declared it was in fact a new path to avoid the landslide.

He changed from his wellies to his shoes, wellies had not been the best choice for the terrain, lacking grip on loose slopes, he chucked them in the boot before phoning Jane at the Pathology department.

"Another one incoming," he said.

"Already here", she answered. "It has got here before you, Prof Rowlands will have a look at it first thing in the morning. Is there anything we need to know about it?" she asked.

"Nothing specific really, I'm assuming it is likely a missing person, though as yet the team haven't linked it to anyone local, however, it is obviously early days, they have only just been told about it in the last hour, they will extend the net over the next couple of days to other force areas. I don't for a minute think there is anything suspicious about it, some poor sod has more than likely come down here to spend his last few hours." Idris Huws was fairly satisfied that the case would be done and dusted in no time at all and that he could get back again to his generally dull policing.

Eight am the next day, dull, dreary and overcast. The ideal weather to be stuck in an autopsy room. Coffee cup in hand, not the nicest either, why couldn't the average machine just produce normal boring coffee like he made at home. He knew he needed to reduce the amount of caffeine he drank drastically, having had a couple of episodes of palpitations that his Gp had put down to too much of the dark blend. He slowly made his way towards the mortuary, dawdling as some would describe it, maybe delaying the inevitable of what was ahead of him. The hospital had expanded hugely since it was first built in the eighties, replacing the original unbelievably small hospital, which stood on a site now housing a supermarket in the student area of the city, it was beyond belief that it could actually have functioned at its size, but then again it had many satellite hospitals around the north-west that people were transferred, to when the acute illness had improved, or more morbidly where they were sent to die, nearer home, and visiting family. Most of these had shut now due to government cuts, so the current edifice on the hill was always full to overflowing. God help anyone needing an ambulance in a rush these days, most of the county's ambulances and crews were stuck for hours, outside the casualty department for lack of space upstairs in the wards. He hoped every time he came here that he would have no need for it himself any time soon. All these random thoughts just slowing his footfall as he approached the double doors to his destination.

Jane was waiting for him, she opened the door that led into the glass-fronted viewing gallery. Rowlands already in the main theatre of gruesome procedures was prepared masked and gloved. A quick nod of acknowledgement as he drew back the sheet as if he was a dramatic magician.

The remains were already stripped of the clothing remnants and footwear, bagged by officers at the scene for investigation.

"Mm," mumbled Rowlands, "Male, around one eight five centimetres." He glanced at Huws, "That's 6 feet to you and me, though I can be a bit more accurate when we have done some measurements, Jane, can you get on with that please." This type of autopsy was not an everyday occurrence for Rowlands, and he didn't quite follow the same procedure as his otherwise daily methods. He would usually have started with a large Y incision to reveal the internal organs, which would have been carefully examined in situ before removal and weighing pre-dissection. This poor sod was basically a collection of bones, barely held together, with rope-like remnants of ligaments, dried out into a dull light green, all tendon tissue and softer muscle and fat long gone, there wasn't even a single maggot anywhere, an empty skull loosely attached to the spinal column totally emptied of its cranial contents, devoured overtime via the eye sockets.

Jane continued with her camera work, concentrating on the skull and its discoloured, tombstone teeth. All the gum tissue was gone, but the skull still had the ability to put on a macabre grin. Huws was thankful at least, that most of the teeth were there, providing a modicum of a chance that some dental record identification investigation might bear fruit. He continued to watch through his glass screen, but needed to stand and move his position for a better view, as well as to stretch his stiffening hip and buttock muscles from the previous day's exertions up the hill from the shore. Both Jane and Emyr Rowlands seemed deep in conversation, closely studying the thigh-bone of the right leg. He pushed the communication button, cleared his throat.

"Anything interesting I should know about?"

"Well, mm, we are just noting some striated marks on the femur bone, but more likely to have happened post-mortem, strange really as the carrion you would expect would be birds, foxes and maybe badgers, but I do know there aren't that many badgers in this immediate area. Could be dog-tooth marks, is it an area where you would get many dogs?"

"No, I wouldn't think so, it's off any direct public footpath really," said Huws.

"OK, likely a fox has had a good gnaw at it too. It's difficult to give a date of death in this case, let alone a time of death with the bones having been bleached clean, and virtually every scrap of flesh stripped off. There are a few tests we can do to try to both age the remains and give an estimation of how long the poor bugger had been there. The fact it was outdoors, exposed to the elements as opposed to buried, is slightly more difficult because some of the tests that are done include histological examination, and reactions between amino acids, degradation of Lipids and so on. Obviously modern Forensic DNA profiling, radio isotopic and radiological techniques will give us a bit more info." Huws nodded knowingly and slightly exaggeratedly aiming to give the impression that he had in fact understood most of what he had just been told, as with most senior officers the minutiae of pathology speak was generally beyond his comprehension. "What I can tell you however is that whoever this is, suffered a fracture of the left femur at some point in their life , probably in the last five years, and has had at least three of his ribs on the same side broken, so maybe a sporting injury, or involvement in a car crash. His teeth looked to have been healthy, with just one amalgam filling in his number 29 tooth lower right." Huws nodded, a little bit to go on for his team to go through the national missing persons list to see if that threw up any clues.

"The results for his age won't take too long, but the length of time he has been there may take a little longer, but in my humble estimation it may well be a year, maybe even a couple of years, so no point looking for a recently missing person."

Huws nodded, and mumbled a thank you as he made to leave, no post pm whisky offered this time.

Chapter Eleven

LIFE CHANGED SLIGHTLY from that day in the village of Allt Goch, and in fact the reverberations of the shocking discovery spread far and wide over the island. It was always said that despite Anglesey being two hundred and seventy-five square miles with a rough population of seventy thousand, it was always said to be the largest village in Wales, despite its many towns and villages. It was a community, particularly for the original inhabitants who had been born and bred within its shoreline, everyone knew each other despite maybe living twenty miles apart. In no time at all, the story was all around the Island, on social media and the local papers, it was gossip and wild speculation about the possible murderer living amongst them. The police were even receiving regular calls from people declaring that they had a 'strangely behaving neighbour'. Nothing yet had been forthcoming from the missing persons list, and the net of the search was spreading beyond the localised area for possibles. That, Idris Huws feared was going to take time. There had been a press release with some details given, it had to be done to stop the local press hounding them, it was one of the things he hated now, social media, it was never an issue when he first joined. You always had a couple of local reporters who you got to know, and largely they reported, to help police not thwart their efforts in an investigation, now there was Facebook, Twitter. And god knows what else. He should know, his daughter's face was glued to her phone screen every chance she got, talked of likes and shares and tweets, all beyond him. Unfortunately, it also caused the police some major problems, due to the fact that, the local papers posted on their social pages, allowing every Tom, Dick and Harry to leave comments, sometimes hundreds of them, causing pain and upset to many families. One of the things he warned his team about constantly, was not to give the papers any information whatsoever referring to anything sensitive until the next of kin were notified, another aspect that wasted manpower on scene now, was having to delegate someone simply to be aware of people taking photos and videos at scenes of accidents, and then immediately putting them onto these various social media platforms. He thought it horrific that next of kin were finding out about the death of relatives via a post online. Times had changed, he doubted very much that it would go back to as it was. He was however quite glad that he was the only IT dinosaur in his team, as the technology they now had available at their fingertips was way beyond him. He seemed to remember that in his last year at secondary school the library room was being reorganized to allow for the introduction of word processors, words such as floppy discs and hard drives being bandied about were way into the future, word processors, if his memory served him right, were just glorified electric typewriters with a screen attached. He wondered if there would be a day when his inability to understand, or in fact refuse to put his mind to it, would mean him not being able to do his job.

Chapter Twelve

SUMMER DAYS SHORTENED INTO AUTUMN, the dominant earthy smells of plants receding into the earth, dropping decaying dried leaves and hunkering down for the winter, filling the air. Rapidly putrifying leaves on the ground releasing their musky sickly sweet smell.

The long days of summer behind now, visitor numbers definitely reducing in Beaumaris, the local town. Blackberry visitors, as his old mum used to call them. That saying, had, when he was a young child, led to a belief, that they visited in order to collect the succulent autumn blackberries, and not the actual time of year when they were ripe. Silverheads, was another description, older people, coach tours making the most of the fact that children had gone back to school and places were generally quiet.

On a miserable rainy day, you could pop to the shop and see no one, a big difference from the hustle and bustle of late spring and summer. The real outdoor enthusiasts enjoyed this short autumnal window before winter set in, to walk the coastal path and visit locations that would previously have been too busy. Anglesey was glorious in good weather, it seemed to have pockets of microclimates, you could always find a place having sunshine whilst others had rain. In winter, it could take on a different identity, ferocious westerlies or easterlies raging across the landscape. Many hedgerow saplings doubled over at ninety degrees cowering from the forces of the prevailing winds, unable to grow straight under its power. There are a few coniferous forests dotted around the island, windblow being an issue with these as well, many of them now under the control of conservation bodies, who no longer managed them for wood production, in the name of protecting some animal species or other. Instead, many which had been previously inaccessible to the public had footpaths woven through them for walkers, cyclists and horse riders. Country parks had opened and old mine workings on the east of the island had paths created for walkers and mountain bikers. The sea was also now a playground not just for the rich and wealthy jet ski, summer noisy invaders, but centres teaching safe kayaking, paddle boarding and coasteering, and such like, it was not surprising therefore, that the population more than quadrupled in a normal year, many a farm outbuilding, converted into bunkhouses and self-catering units, creating extra income to make up for ever reducing income from farming, apart from the very biggest enterprises.

Philip Morrison pulled his hood further over his head tugging the elastic drawstring shorter. So short that only his eyes and nose were visible, peering out of the hood. He had set off through the forestry on Mynydd Llwydiarth in bright sunshine and blue skies, but the rain had soon set in and seemed to be settled to stay for the whole day. The hills of Snowdonia sending over its share of heavy rain. The tree tops towering above him, were doing a seductive swaying dance, in the wind, like a thousand witches brooms, reaching for the skies. The main track through the forestry would take him eventually out to the main road, towards the village of Pentraeth, but he had no plans to go that far today, just a general meander through the woods, which were still relatively unfamiliar to him.

He had only recently moved into the area a few months before. His wife Mary, had not long died, after a long drawn-out painful battle with an inoperable cancerous brain tumour. He hadn't made many new friends in the village yet. They had started the purchase of their new house before she got poorly, and subsequently diagnosed. He had wanted to defer the move, so as not to cause her anymore anxiety than needed, while she was having what turned out to be futile treatment. She was having none of it, she pushed him to proceed and they duly moved. In fact, it worked out well, in the last few weeks, the most dedicated palliative care team stepped in from the local hospital trust, and with the aid of the most fabulous Macmillan nurse towards the end, Mary had the death she wanted, if there is such a thing. Once she knew that there was no more treatment and that she was terminal, she planned everything, taking everything out of his hands, knowing he would unlikely be able to cope by himself. There were no children to worry about, that was a choice they had made when they got married 28 years previously. Their parents were both alive then, and although nothing was said, they both felt that they were considered selfish, to not produce grandchildren to be doted over. Neither of them was particularly child minded, they enjoyed their time together, their activity-filled holidays at home and abroad. They compared this freedom with some of their friend's lives, who seemed to have lost their own, but had melted into a routine of doing child orientated things, which mainly pleased the children. Maybe they themselves were selfish, but it was their choice at the end of the day. Now the love of his life, and very best friend was gone. Life, had changed for him beyond recognition when she went, that terrible day when he sat at her bedside listening to her breaths getting shallower and shallower, until a final exhalation, took her away from him forever. The aftermath of Mary's death had been a blur of organising death certificates, sorting out bank accounts from joint accounts to just his, the funeral which was a green burial in a willow basket casket. Neither of them religious, so friends had been asked to say a few words at the simple ceremony. This was held on the mainland in one of the few places allowed to do this. He had been unsure of the location initially but had been persuaded by Mary that there was no need for him to make a weekly pilgrimage, to visit the graveside which would in fact be a newly planted sapling, to draw on her decaying body as fertiliser, and he was, she had told him, under no circumstances to buy flowers, which were very expensive and would simply rot. This was Mary to the core, realistic and simple. She had told him that her spirit would be with him everywhere he went, and that he was to try his best to find himself another partner, as he would certainly starve to death or eat rubbish without her there. They had these conversations in the last few weeks of her life, and although they found they could laugh at her ideas at the time, the reality of it had left him a totally broken man. Life had changed, he had changed, local people had initially made an attempt to make friends and invite him into their community, but everything he had done before had been with Mary, he wasn't one for Choir singing, book clubs or anything like that, he walked, and walked, and walked. He was a web builder by trade, and since Mary's death, his days had no routine, no timetable, no normality. He got up late, normally after a sleepless night, skipped breakfast or ate an inevitably overripe banana, the healthy diet sheet produced for him by Mary for when she had gone, a long-forgotten memory, his appetite had seemingly died along with his wife. He walked the coastline and local area, returning home at dusk, to then sit until the early hours dealing with work e-mails and design requests. He appreciated, it must be frustrating for clients that he didn't respond to mail, until they had likely been asleep for hours. No doubt he had lost clients by his erratic business patterns. He didn't particularly care. Friends from their previous life had drifted away, he had become unsociable, morose, humourless, choosing not to use social media, preferring to look at the caller's name on his mobile phone, often choosing not to answer, dependent on how he felt at that precise moment. How he felt was in fact rubbish, he did not really want to go on, he was an incomplete person without Mary besides him. Totally fed up to the back teeth of people asking how he was doing. Initially, he would just nod and mumble an OK, but in all honesty he really felt like screaming at them, "How the hell do you think I feel, I've lost the only person in the world I well and truly loved, I feel like shit, all the time, every hour, every day", but he never did say this. It was not their fault.

He walked on along the gravelled track, there were two properties that he had come across in this forest, as far as he could tell, one which had some pretty ferocious dogs running outside, and thankfully a sturdy looking gate. He'd not actually seen anyone there, so he was unsure of the property status. The rain was increasing now, so instead of continuing along the track, he chose to turn off to his left, seeing a well-trodden path veer off amongst the trees. Pine cones and newly fallen needles littered the ground, which was firm underneath his feet, no bogs here like lower down towards the beach, trees creaked and groaned around him, straining against the wind, whipping and weaving through the trunks, some having already succumbed and fallen, causing him to have to scramble over the odd one and duck under others. One tree was totally devoid of bark, virtually hollowed out, it looked like a discarded wasp nest, so damaged was it, from years of endless drilling by a woodpecker. It had clearly been determined. Remains of ancient damp moss covered stone walls occasionally crossed the path, the only remnants of the past existence of smallholding boundaries of long ago, long abandoned when a rich landowner was made an offer they couldn't refuse by the forestry commission, did that still exist he wondered.

He and Mary had both hated the forestation of hills, after a trip to the highlands of Scotland one January, where they saw dozens of dead deer, just above a forestry fence line, they had not been able to get through to lower ground for food or water, all the mountain streams up high had been frozen. He remembered there had been uproar about it at the time, apparently this was no longer allowed to happen. More recent visits had been more pleasing, they had seen large herds of deer on lower ground below the forests, some herds even wandering the village streets in some of the more remote west coast corners. How they loved those holidays. It was strange that to one person, deer could be a means to financial benefits, and to others a cause of misery as they ate everyone's vegetable plots. They couldn't win either way. This was how his brain worked now, random thoughts popping into his head, taking him off on tangents all over the place, it affected his work too. On one hand he despaired, on another he didn't quite honestly care. He didn't really care now what anyone thought of him.

The area up ahead seemed to brighten a little, more sky showing through, a clearing, the canopy opening to the sky which was still grey and full of imminent rain, he pushed on, suddenly ahead, as if dropped there, a chimney stack rose out of the ruinous bed of concrete and bricks, the remains of a house? Was this maybe the old local estate's summer residence that he had heard of. Certainly not much of it left now, a brick-built gable with a long-empty fireplace stood at the opposing side, random ironwork and decayed sheets of tin, from what likely had been a mainly a wooden built chalet type house. Glancing to his left he saw through the bramble-covered undergrowth, a glimpse of open water. Clearly, this was the boathouse spoken of. On closer inspection, it may have been in its time a substantially sized lake, but now bulrushes and reed beds stretched out into the water, choking its surface and reducing its actual surface area. Ducks galore swam gracefully across away from his direction, surprised at having human intrusion and their peace disturbed. A single swan could be seen in the distance, possibly a mate would be sheltering on a reed nest somewhere. Although it was too late in the year he thought to produce a clutch of eggs. Maybe the mate had succumbed to another sadder fate.

There was no defined path around the lake that he could make out, he squinted to improve his focus, but no clear pathway beyond the lake was visible, not unless he wanted to get his feet wetter than they already were.

He stepped back towards the concrete chalet base, put down his small backpack and took out his water container. The wind still hooleyed around him, he felt that the rain was not quite as bad now, or else he was largely protected by the tree canopy overhead. Other than the wind there was no other sound to be heard. Too far from the road for traffic, not enough birdlife other than the odd quack and the sound of beating wings against water, as one either landed or took off.

He heard an occasional crackle of twigs around him, more than likely rabbits in the undergrowth scuttling about their daily business, or maybe a fox. There were supposedly lots of Red squirrels in this particular wood, initially part of a local release programme, but now apparently doing well, though he had never caught sight of one, possibly because walking along staring at your feet, deep in thought did not make the best of what was around him. He had, he thought seen a couple of feeder boxes on a couple of trees not long after he left the track. Someone must be monitoring them. The sky above the canopy was to his surprise brightening now, blue with mackerel clouds, the pine tips having paused in their seductive swaying dance. Philip Morrison pushed back his hood, and rubbed his dampened hair off his forehead. Just ahead was a rivulet, a crude bridge created across it by a fallen trunk. He knew that people came here with their mountain bikes, and actually created a few routes criss-crossing the forest, he had no issue with this, as they were at least quiet, compared to the moto-cross bikes, that seemed to enjoy cutting up the saltings, far below him on the edge of the beach, they plagued the local residents on summer evenings with their silencer-less exhaust noise and excessive revving. They did a fair bit of damage to the eco-system. He stepped onto the log, damp with lichen and fungi, he almost lost his balance, then found his footing again.

Suddenly all the air was forced out of him in a strangled gasp, something pushed him hard from behind, sprawling scissor legged astride the log, his whole body involuntarily tensed against a heavy unrelenting weight. His face was pressed down into the stream bed, only literally an inch, no more, of sour pine needle-filled brackish water, but nevertheless filling his airways as he was grabbed tightly from behind around his neck. Please, please let me go, he thought, as his life blood ebbed away into the now dark crimson stream, running down to join the very lake he had just been admiring. Had he still been alive, he would have heard a loud cacophony of sounds, as all the birds in the surrounding area erupted out of the waters to escape whatever had created the surrounding disturbance. They soon returned and a peace once again descended on the area .

Chapter Thirteen

DI HUWS CLEARED his throat for attention, simply entering the hall had not worked, all heads down, some on the phone, some typing away, one busy at a map of the UK sticking coloured pins in what at least appeared to be a purposeful fashion. "Right, you lot, what do we have here, Unrhyw Lwc?" As he reverted to his native welsh language. "Anyone had any luck with anything useful?? He looked around, as he put one bum cheek on the corner of the desk, where a young police officer sat. He wondered if she had even actually moved at all, since he had seen them last. She looked up at him.

"Well, the Missing Persons Bureaux has come up with five possibles for the description we have, we have already discounted three of them so far, but are still looking into the other two, we are in contact with next of kin, so hopefully we will have some news on those by the end of the day."

"OK, good work," he recognised the enthusiasm in her that he had as a young rookie, as soon as he had found his feet . Policing was very different these days, and in his opinion, not always in a good way, too many interferers higher up the social scale, too many do-gooder's believing in the rehabilitation of offenders, when he knew all along that most of them were bad apples, despite any guidance they might be given. In his day a clip around the ear would have dealt with most minor offenders, but woe betide you did that now. No, things had gone seriously astray in the judicial system, and sadly these young officers in this room would likely soon find this out and soon sour. The Force lost so many keen young officers nowadays when they realised just how far around their backs their hands were tied.

"OK, so back to young Sarah, have we made any headway there at all? Any luck with the house-to-house visits?"

"No, not really," said a voice from the back of the room. "Nothing to go on that had any solidity, a couple of cottage owners declaring their last guests as odd, but nothing more than 'not smiling back at them and being unsociable', though that particular lady, would no doubt have your life story off you in ten minutes given the opportunity, the visitors probably hid when they saw her approaching." Subdued laughter rose in the room. There would be very few people holidaying in the area at the moment who were single. This was still just about school holiday time so families filled the streets and beaches. "So,I take it no one has had any loners staying?"

"We still have a couple of cottage owners to catch up with, but they live away, and deal with the bookings themselves as opposed to using an agency. Mind you we did have a chat with a couple of local ladies who do the changeover cleaning too, though their main concern seemed to be the people who left the grill pan filthy, and left skid marks in the toilet bowl," said Howard. "These cleaning ladies however, rarely see the guests as they have left before they arrive to clean, and they in turn have gone before the next guests come in".

"Thank you for your efforts so far, but we really need to get on with this now, pressure is building up and time is of the essence. We have heard however that there is no evidence whatsoever that she was sexually assaulted in any way, so that is clearly not a motive, and I'm sure in a small way it will be a relief to her parents, but, whoever attacked her used something which was clearly not a sharp knife, but something which caused massive lacerations, torn wounds, a total nutter clearly. Also, at this point in time there is very little to link the two bodies, one clearly very recent, and the other we are not sure yet, that information is dependent on test results, but clearly a fair time ago, but let's not discount anything." He was desperate for a cigarette, but had stopped smoking a while ago, his vape had to do. He walked out of the hall straight out onto the deserted roadway outside, the hall was right next door to the village pub, he could just sink a pint, but it had instilled into him as a young pc, not to ever go to the local pub, apparently, he would lose respect in the community or so his seniors at the time drilled into him. Old-fashioned beliefs, he reckoned it might be one of the best places to get some seeds of information. Now, despite him actually not having been in uniform for years, it was a habit he had never broken-as yet.

He pulled on his vape as he strolled to his right towards the main village, releasing a cloud of white vapour in his trail, the road to his left wound its way steeply down a hill to the beach, and in fact a footpath off this hill would have led him to the now taped off scene of crime, which was still subject to a fingertip search. He shut his eyes and shook his head, still seeing the terrible scenes that had been in front of him, both at the scene and at the mortuary, he shook his head in despair, at the capabilities of someone to be sick enough in the head, to be able to carry out such an act. He ventured as far as the bus stop, decorated with pretty knitted bunting, not something he had seen before, maybe it was a village thing.

A stooped man was ambling slowly up the road, head down, clearly no intention of making eye contact.

"Diwrnod braf," said Huws, more a question than a statement, hoping for a response, this seemed to catch the man out, possibly not expecting a stranger in his village to speak welsh, he hesitated, as he drew alongside on the other side of the road.

"Da chi yn byw yma?" asked Huws, simply asking if he was a local.

"Pwy sy'n gofyn? Who is asking?" he replied, with a defensive tone to his voice. Huws introduced himself, and crossed the road towards him. The man's face immediately took on a distinct look of suspicion or guilt, a look that sometimes appeared even if they had been paragons of virtue all their lives.

"I'm here with my team, investigating the tragic murder of a young lady, that took place the other day."

"Yes I know," he mumbled quietly. "You won't find the animal capable of doing that here in this village."

"Possibly not, but we have to follow every avenue possible to bring this to the conclusion it deserves". He slipped a card out of his wallet and passed it to the man. "Do you have a name? It's good to get to know a few of the locals."

He would in his mind, immediately label the man standing in front of him as a quiet loner, and certainly not a criminal. He seemed a little hesitant to divulge his name, but eventually mumbled, "Iorwerth, Iorwerth Davies. Only an animal could do that to the poor girl", he almost whispered, as he took the card out of Huws's hand, stuffing it into his back pocket without even a glance. Iorwerth Davies walked straight into the pub, pulling the door tightly behind him, a sign thought Huws that he and his like were far from welcome. Huws nodded to himself in response to the man's answer, then put his vape in his pocket. He never found them as satisfying as a decent Benson and Hedges.

He walked around to the back of the pub, where one of the team had asked to park a few of the squad cars, two young lads were sitting atop a picnic bench watching him., with slight disdain.

"Do you know who killed Sarah yet?" asked the red-headed chubby lad.

"Doing our best," answered Huws. He needed to check on the forensics team at scene, and then visit the girl's parents to see if he could find anything more than his DS had already done.

Chapter Fourteen

DAWN TIED Bella's lead rein to the ring on the wall, and reached down into the grooming kit box for a body brush and curry comb, she loved the horse's coats at this time of year, soft and silky with a natural shine provided by good grass and sunshine. Soon it would start to thicken slightly and get a bit dull as the winter coat started to push through.

   She couldn't remember a time when she didn't ride, or in fact didn't live in the forestry, not a single main road did she have to venture along if she chose not too, unless she took the track to the lane that led to the vast expanse of beach, that was locally called Red Wharf bay. The section of beach that she used, was called Wern y Wylan beach, after the little hamlet just up the hill. It wasn't that popular with holidaymakers, as the tide went so far out, it was a pain to walk out far enough to have sufficient depth to swim. Many a happy afternoon she had spent here on young ponies and horses over the years, exposing them to a wide expanse of open space, paddling in the sea, jumping up and down banks on the salting's as well as the exhilarating gallops she had enjoyed. This was something she had educated herself about over the years, always walk the track you intend to gallop first, in one direction, just to double check that there were no tendon tearing soft patches, which would suck a horse's leg in up to the knees and catch out the unwary reckless rider. Many a horse had badly injured itself hereabouts. Dawn took her time grooming, teasing out the ringlets in Bella's mane, always a nuisance with these welsh cobs, that tended to have a long thick mane, they twisted in the breeze, tails the same. This aspect of being with her horses gave her just as much pleasure as the actual riding, she had a choice of a few to ride, she had always taken an interest in breeding a few over the years, so most of the horses were related to each other, and were broken to ride when they reached the age for it.

She knew the forest surrounding her home like the back of her hand, every path and dead- end track of it, every fallen log that she had used as a cross-country fence when younger, though someone, and she suspected, it may be a local mountain bike enthusiast, had cleared some of these aside in recent years. She lifted the saddle off the stable door next to her, placing it forwards on Bella's wither and gently sliding it back into position, pulling the saddle cloth up into the gullet of the pommel, so as not to create pressure. She gently drew the girth from underneath Bella's tummy, and pulled hard to reach the straps with the buckle, it was always a competition between them, Bella blowing her tummy out as much as she could, in order for the girth to only just reach. At this point, Dawn would put on the bridle, gently lifting the metal bit up to Bella's tightly closed teeth, which always relented with the gentle insertion of a thumb into the corner of her mouth, and gentle pressure on her gums. It was never an argument between them, just a game Bella had always played. By the time Dawn had stuffed her hair inside her riding helmet and released Bella from her knot on the wall, Bella would have forgotten to blow out her tummy, and Dawn could do up the girth. It would need doing again once she had ridden a few hundred yards. She drew Bella alongside the step platform her father had built for her and her siblings many moons ago, though at that age she was able to gracefully vault onto her ponies. Not so nimble now. She grasped the reins in her left hand as she put her left toe in the nearside stirrup, reached over to the far side of the pommel and swung herself over, simultaneously finding the right stirrup. Bella was not the most patient of mares, liking to be up and off as soon as Dawn's bum touched the saddle.

Yesterday's wind and rain had cleared, some trees could still be heard to creak in the breeze. Rarely were they totally still, but she loved the green tones showing themselves as the sun speckled through the trees, more shades of green than she could even imagine there were names for. Bella swung along in her low ground covering stride, like being atop a big sofa, thought Dawn smiling to herself. She had her most interesting conversations when she was out riding, very one-sided clearly, but her horses knew all her innermost secrets, hopes and wishes. They ambled on, reins in one hand, no contact with Bella's soft as velvet mouth, consequently she was able to plunge her head down and grab at some tall grasses alongside the track, creating a mass of green slather and spittle, that she would then spray all over Dawn, as she either snorted or tossed her head to dislodge an imagined fly. Dawn always used her time whilst riding, daydreaming, making grand plans for her future, which actually wasn't very different from the life she currently lived in the forest now, with her ageing parents. She did worry a little about how her parents might cope with this location as they got older, but thankfully currently they were fit and well albeit a little less active. She gently lay the right rein across Bella's neck, encouraging her to yield to the pressure, and move across off the gravel road onto a path. She liked this track, as the organisation which had taken on the responsibility of reintroducing the red squirrels into the forest, had feeders here and thereabouts on various trees. Perspex fronted peanut-filled boxes with lids that the squirrels knew somehow to lift to access the nut supply. If she stood here quietly enough for a while, she regularly saw the beautiful russet-coloured creatures go about their daily routines. It seemed that they were not in the least bit perturbed about a big lump of a horse being on their territory, and seemed oblivious of the human perched atop. She would laugh to herself when the odd squirrel actually found the lid close above its head, whilst stuffing its cheeks with nuts, and for a few seconds would look pathetically out of the perspex before realising all it had to do was give a gentle upward push. She never ever however seemed to be able to get her mobile phone out quickly enough, to get a really decent photo, before they were sprinting vertically up the trees into the canopy. She reached the squirrel clearing but there seemed to be no one busy feeding there today. She had learnt that the place to look was in fact way above her head in the tree canopy, they normally built their drays a fair way up, often in the branches of a fork in the trunk. There could be a whole motorway of activity going on above people's heads, when they came looking for these elusive creatures, but so busy were they looking at the feeders and the ground, they inevitably missed the activity above. She gave up today, shortened the reins a touch and gently squeezed her heels against Bella's side. There is nothing better than a Welsh cob for picking its way along rough ground. A little bit like an all- terrain vehicle or four-wheel drive. She knew this particular path was a dead end, but she loved seeing the remnants of the old farm walls, now toppled higgledy-piggledy and covered in a thick verdant moss, always damp and holding water regardless of how dry it had been. There had been five small farms on this hillside at one time, but theirs and next door were the only ones remaining, with another further along the hill towards Allt Goch, none of which were now farmed, it had almost been akin to the Highland Clearances when the present local lord's father had it all planted in the fifties. A couple of old ruined cottages could still be found if you knew where to look for them. She could also now smell the nearby lake, the slightly putrid smell of decaying waterside vegetation. The local gentry used to swim and fish in it apparently, many moons ago but in her lifetime and probably far longer, it had just lain unused, unmanaged and reverting to nature, closing itself down at its edges to any chance of human recreation. Bella tensed under her, her normally flabby fat-covered muscles taking on a quiver all of their own. She stopped, and despite a nudge forwards by Dawn, she rooted herself to the spot and stood her ground. She grew from her normal fifteen hands to seventeen, so much was the tension growing in every nerve of her body. She snorted, her ears pricked and rotated like a radar dish, listening out for whatever she clearly thought was out to get her. It was unlike Bella to do this, normally the most laid back and basically laziest of horses.

"Come on old girl," said Dawn, a laugh in her tone. "What's got you today?" Without warning Bella span her body around on her haunches, lowering herself, creating such centrifugal force, that Dawn found herself slammed against the nearest tree trunk, which frightened Bella all the more, causing her to leap away leaving Dawn to fall heavily in the gap left between the terrified mare's shoulders and the tree. Dawn was thumped into the ground all the air pushed out of her body winding her, making her gasp like a dying fish,

"Oh Woah, woah," she shouted, knowing really that shouting would not help in the least, but Bella was showing her a clean pair of heels as she disappeared towards the way they came, stirrups flying, the heavy metal banging on her sides with every stride, only adding to her perceived fright, at whatever she had imagined she had seen.

Dawn looked around for her glasses, or at least felt around on the mossy ground, without her glasses on her face she couldn't see to find the actual glasses. Thankfully they were just to the right of her, and better still undamaged. Dawn however, quickly realised that she must have cut herself, there was blood on her hand. She wasn't too worried about Bella running off, there was no actual traffic to worry about, the two forest exits were gated and she knew she would find her way home, though she cursed the long walk home that she had to make.

Dawn wiped her hand on her jumper and looked to see what damage she had done, she stared for a moment bemused, surprised to find no cuts, she then felt her face and imagined she must have a nosebleed but no, nothing, twisting around to see the backs of her legs. She saw that where she had clearly made contact with the ground, there was blood on her clothing. It was only at this point that it occurred to her to look where she fell. Open-mouthed and in disbelief, she saw that the ground near the tree was actually a dark crimson, a soaked in puddle of blood, how could that have happened when she hadn't actually hurt herself. Had she had some sort of sinister haemorrhage, had Bella struck into herself and was now heading home with a fatal bleed!

There was no phone signal in the forest, so she knew trying to phone her dad to beg a lift was out of the question, so it was to be a long walk home, or they would see Bella by the gate without her and set off by car to look for her. It wasn't the first time in her life it had happened. She made to set off, dusting herself down, assuming from the scuff marks around her were Bella's hooves and probably the fox that had clearly had a rabbit kill earlier. Being surrounded by foxes she was used to their scent and rabbit remains though she was quite surprised that Bella had reacted as she had.

Suddenly a splash of colour caught her eye beyond the tree, it was a small backpack, the type she herself sometimes used if she walked along the beach and around the block, she leant down and picked it up. Looking around for a possible owner she opened the zip, feeling a bit like a thief, inside was a Mars Bar and small water bottle, the flask type that keeps water cold. There was also a rolled up lightweight rain coat. Shouting out, "Hello is there anyone around? Are you OK"? She listened for an answer, peering through the trees around her. A raindrop fell landing on her cheek, she instinctively wiped it away.

"Oh my god," she almost shouted to herself as she brushed at her cheek, and stared at her hand. Disbelief!

"Blood," this time she looked up, and froze.

"Jesus Christ almighty," she said, not that she was in the least bit religious. High up above her head was a man, at least she assumed it was a man by his clothing, seemingly hanging off a bough around twenty feet above her head, that was clearly what Bella had seen or sensed. He appeared fully dressed but blood-soaked. She couldn't see his face properly, she didn't want to, she was already jogging away along the path as fast as her legs could carry her, and could get her breath. She reached the gravel track, thank god downhill from here. She heard shouting!

"Dad, dad!" Unaware almost that it was actually her own screaming echoing back at her through the trees, no one answered, no one came, she ran, the last corner ahead of her now before she turned off the main track towards her home, she shouted again, this time her father's head appearing above the gate. Bella was still there, no one had noticed her appearance.

"What the hell are you shouting at?" said Eric, seemingly not even aware that his daughter and her horse, had made their way home separately and under their own steam.

"Dad, there is a person hanging in a tree, not far from the lake, they must have killed themself, there is blood everywhere around the tree, I fell in it, Bella refused to go and span around dumping me over her shoulder." All this was coming out like verbal diarrhea, in between great gasps of breath and tears. "OK, OK, OK, calm down. Let's just get this mare in and we will phone the police. Listen, I will put her in, and untack her, you go indoors, you look like shit." Eric was never one to mince his words, tough, ex-forces, seen a few horrors in his time. Dawn hastened towards the house, bursting through the back door and falling in a disheveled weeping heap into the old dog's armchair in the kitchen, surprising her old mum Pat.

"Hi Love, you OK? You look as white as a sheet, are you not well, I thought you were out riding?"

It all poured out of Dawn like a river of panic, as the enormity of what she had seen hit her, alongside the bruising soreness that was now creeping up her right side as often happened after a fall, adrenaline coursing through a body initially, before it reduced and revealed the real intensity of pain. Her poor old mum stood open-mouthed.

"Hung themselves, here? Poor soul, here let me just get you a cup of tea, your hands are shaking, poor love. How awful for you." Eric stepped in through the door.

"Have you phoned the police?"

"No, of course not yet, give us a chance, Dawn is very upset," scolded Pat. Eric grabbed the hand's free phone off the sideboard and dialled 999. He explained to the police that he would need to drive to the forest entrance to unlock the barrier for them, and would meet them there with Dawn who could then show them where this person was.

"Oh no dad, I don't want to go there again, I don't want to see it." Dawn begged her father. She couldn't face it again.

"You won't need to look, but you can lead us down the path as close as you feel comfortable, come on, it won't take them long to get here from Llangefni, they said they would send someone straight away." He urged Dawn onto her feet and in a totally uncharacteristic move he hugged his daughter, Dawn wasn't sure if this almost shocked her as much as finding someone hanging from a tree. Eric ushered his still upset daughter towards the car and went to open the gate. He was a battle-hardened man, and this sort of news off his daughter was in all honesty, water off a ducks back to him, yes, some poor sod had felt the need to do this to himself for reasons known only to himself, but he was mainly concerned always, with keeping his own family safe and secure, and would in all honesty go out of his way to protect them in any way he needed to. It was one of the reasons he had moved them to this place, many moons ago now, and raised his children in its natural cocoon. The one thing that had given him a bit of a shake, was a purposefully started forest fire in the early 90's, that had taken ten days to properly be extinguished. That had created a vulnerability that stupidly he hadn't planned for, but thankfully the culprit had been found and arrested.

Dawn sat in silence for the almost two-mile drive to the barrier, just glancing to her left as she passed the mouth of the path she had followed, shivering at the thought of the poor person hanging there. Why there she thought, it would now forever be tainted with the vision of what she had seen, she would never be able go down that path again. Eric opened the barrier, securing it back to the post then swung the car around in the entrance, to park up and wait for the police. They sat in silence, he had never been good with all the tea and sympathy stuff, Pat had always been the one for that sort of stuff, he chose to just sit and stare, and lift his eyes to the rear-view mirror when a vehicle went past the entrance.

On some days the entrance sides were filled with parked cars, usually people keen to catch a glimpse of the forest's elusive red squirrel colony. He had by now seen so man, the novelty had worn off. A car swung in behind him, a local panda car. He didn't waste his time getting out to acknowledge their presence, he simply raised his hand and drove on. They would know to follow.

"This path, next on the right?" he asked Dawn as they had covered a mile or so, the panda car behind them quickly backing off his tail to avoid the blinding cloud of dust that rose from the trucks off-road wheels. She nodded. He pulled up the vehicle, no effort to pull in, only they as a family regularly used the road, if the holiday home residents next door came along, they could damn well wait.

"I'm not coming," said Dawn. "You go, keep to the path, over the old field wall and it's a bit further than the little stream."

"Ok, I'll show them," he answered as he did his coat zip up, his little effort maybe to look slightly tidier and more presentable.

"Don't forget you are not looking for them on the ground, they are quite high up in a tree." Dawn, a sob breaking out involuntarily, closed her eyes as the vision of the poor person again appeared in front of her. Unfortunately, it seemed that the image was also etched inside her eyelids. Shutting her eyes had not helped.

Eric strode off briskly as was his habit, he never walked slowly anywhere, he was followed hot on his heels by two uniformed policemen who appeared to be tipping along avoiding getting their boots dirty. Dawn stared ahead, watching them disappear out of sight, knowing that in less than thirty seconds they would see the man. Her whole environment was forever somehow soured and spoilt.

The sun was in the West at tree top-level now, causing Dawn to squint as spears of sunlight broke through the now gently swaying treetops. The day had improved into the afternoon, what an awful thing to do to yourself on such a nice day she thought, contemplating what awful things must have happened to this person to make them do such a thing to themselves. Suddenly, the door opened and Eric slid back in beside her.

"I've been asked to leave the scene," he announced as he turned the key in the ignition.

"Well, actually I've been asked to go and get a ladder for them. It is a man, but he isn't hanging, he is sort of wedged in a fork, they have sent for back- up." "Wow," said Dawn, why would anyone be climbing the trees? Whatever he was doing he has clearly slipped, poor bloke, but what a stupid thing to be doing."

They set off along the track towards home, a sudden horrible thought occurred to Dawn.

"Is he actually dead? Oh, Christ! What if he isn't and I just went off and left him, that would be awful, I might have been able to help."

"Don't be daft," said Eric, "How the hell were you supposed to actually get up the tree to do anything about it, the old mare probably smelt him, and then probably caught a glimpse of him above, you know what horses are like, despite domestication for centuries, they still expect to see a lion around every corner, and their single and only instinct is to run, run first look later, you should know that by now." He whistled out his breath between his teeth.

"Open the gate gal," seemingly now Dawn's despair and upset to be forgotten. He had raised them tough.

Chapter Fifteen

DI HUWS SAT in the store room, that had been allocated to him as a makeshift office in the community centre, mops and buckets and cleaning fluids moved aside, and the smallest table he had ever seen as a desk. He hadn't asked for an office, but had been ushered into here by Pete Smith, who seemed determined to get him away from the rest of the team while they worked, probably because, by his own admission he could be a bit of a tyrant. He had just come off the phone with headquarters at Llangefni, a couple of uniform guys had just phoned from a forestry, a few miles east, a simple hanging is what they were expecting, but they apparently needed a team there right now, it was far from simple, they had got up to him, a local with a ladder had helped, but had immediately realised there was a fair bit more to it than first thought. The guy was indeed suspended up a tree, but seemingly there was no sign of hanging, he was wedged in a fork, and had been brutally attacked, his throat gaping open, and indeed could not be identified as his face was virtually torn away. Llangefni had added that the two bobbies were in a bit of a state, and had in fact left the scene, they were now both sitting in the car on the main track, locked themselves in by all accounts. They had told them to, "Bloody well get back to the scene," at which the reply was, "Well, no one really goes down there anyway," to which they reiterated, "Well some people clearly do, as there is a guy up a tree who now has no face." Huws listened to all this information, he had written down basic notes, he now needed to tell his team that they had body number three in almost as many days.

Something didn't sit well with him about this, too many connections, similarities to the young girl maybe, and only a few days later. He didn't like it, he really didn't like what this was starting to look like, though he was reasonably happy that the skeletal remains that were found was a timing coincidence and likely an old suicide. More than likely , a thorough trawl through the National Database of missing persons would find the skeletons earthly owner. Llangefni had already made contact with SOCO and they were on their way. He entered the main office, about to tap a desk to draw their attention when a young female pc cut his plan short.

"I think we may know who the remains belong to. A forty-five year old male who went missing from Dyffryn near Barmouth in early 2017, he had a history of depression, was five foot eleven, his trainers match how he was dressed when he was last seen by his Mother, he told her he was going off into the hills to 'Get his head round stuff', something he did quite often, she added, he had history of going walkabout off grid, without telling anyone where he was going, or how long for. He was wearing a shirt that matched the few torn remnants on his body, but she had no idea of the make at the time he was reported missing. She didn't report him missing for a week, because it's what he did. He refused to carry a mobile phone with him, because he believed people were out to get him. He had however supposedly taken his supply of medication, it was not left in his room; He was a registered schizophrenic. There was an extensive search for him following her eventually reporting him as missing. Our colleagues in that area have just confirmed that he was considered a vulnerable person, they had also involved a couple of their more local mountain and lowland rescue teams, concentrating mainly on the mainland in his local area, he was known to use busses and would often hitch a lift. Most of the locals would pick him up and drop him off.

There was no harm in him, more a danger to himself than others. No searches were made for him at the time on Anglesey, but Griff is following up the CCTV footage from the Menai Bridge, to see if anyone matching his description had walked across, but we aren't holding our breath because so many students from the University and just locals in general cross it every day, unless he crossed it at night, which makes spotting someone a bit easier, it's a bit of a needle in a haystack job. But they will see if they come up with anything. We are quite confident though that it is our skeleton."

She had barely taken a breath whilst telling Huws this information, all without looking at a single note, she was keen fair play thought Huws.

"That's Great," he said, now he could get a word in edgeways; having once been the keen bright young copper himself until cynicism got in the way, he understood his young officer's enthusiasm.

"Right, the team working on the scene of Sarah Jones's murder have finished there with nothing new to report, however I have just moved them on, not far away in fact as the crow flies, less than two miles. We had a young horse-rider who has come across a male victim of an attack, who somehow or other has been put up into a tree, we have absolutely no idea as yet how or why he was up there, but the first reports coming back are that he has been the victim of a vicious assault. Whoever has done this has clearly been in a frenzy, there are lots of similarities in the wounds inflicted I'm told."

Idris Huws paused to allow the news to sink in.

There was a sharp intake of breath to be heard around the room.

"Shit," he heard one of the lads say. "Is this connected to Sarah Jones do you think? It sounds as if the same instrument may have been used."

"We don't know yet, they are preparing to get him out of the tree at the moment, and securing the scene, we will know more when we get him to the pathologist."

Chapter Sixteen

CAROLINE WAS JUST EMPTYING the contents of a pooper scooper into the wheelbarrow, when the yard phone rang. She walked to the feed room door where the phone was set up on the wall and answered.

"Hi," is all she got out as the voice at the other end hissed down the line.

"There is a big cat in your bottom fields, get here now."
　　No way did she have any ideas who this was at the other end, they seemed to be talking strangely. Was it some sort of scammer?

"Who is this, what did you say about a cat?" The voice hissed again, though a little more slowly.

. . .

Community Killing

"It's Tom, from along the beach, I'm on the bottom slope of my field on my tractor, topping, I'm able to see your water meadow at the bottom, there is a big cat in there, I've just seen it spray up a tree, It's huge. I'm whispering because I don't want it to see me. I don't want to attract attention to myself. I have no protection from it on this tractor, it hasn't got a cab. I've phoned the police before I phoned you, though I don't hold out much hope of them coming here any time soon. They wanted a grid reference and stuff, I don't tend to carry a map on my tractor. Do you have a shotgun?"

Caroline could only stare at the phone when Tom hung up abruptly. She could barely believe what she had just heard.

"James," she shouted as she ran past the barn and up the slope towards the cottage, "James," louder, she knew it was pretty pointless expecting him to appear promptly, he wasn't too good on his pins these days. She flung open the back door and there he stood, oblivious to her shouts, drying the dishes, he had not heard her shouts.

"Quick, we need to get down to the beach fields, Tom's just phoned from there and says there is a big cat in the field."
"What colour?" asked James as if that really mattered, he could have been referring to a pussy cat.

"My god does it really matter? I didn't think to ask Tom, it's a big cat as in a wild cat, just go and get your shotgun out of the cabinet," she said marching towards the car.

"Seems sad to shoot it," said James, as he turned towards the stairs to fetch his gun out of the gun cabinet, for a minute he had forgotten where the key was, but once he found it under the pile of pillowcases on the nearby shelf, he then couldn't remember for the life of him, when he had last used it. As he stuffed some cartridges out of the box into his waistcoat pocket, he could hear the car outside the house now, Caroline purposely doing wheel spins up the gravel slope towards the cottage, and revving the engine making it plain that she wanted him to hurry.

He hobbled down the stairs, he was in desperate need of a new hip but having a history of a heart attack in ninety- four he wasn't keen to go under the knife. He grabbed the roof handle and hoisted himself into the car, bum cheek at a time, and shuffled to face forwards, shutting the door to as Caroline was already setting off down the track, gravel flying behind them. Caroline paused at the drive entrance just to check there was no one coming off the beach to the left. The main road was a dead end at their entrance, theirs being the last property on this stretch of road, only the beach track opening out onto Red Wharf bay below the farm. The other properties were accessed from the Pentraeth side by a beach road, flooded at high tide.

She drove the familiar twists and turns, up the hill, knowing by instinct where she may meet another car. She was by now, having had a lot of practise, having met hundreds of incapable drivers able to reverse almost as quickly as she could drive forwards, if necessary. They reached the village, turned left and continued past the pub and down the Allt Goch hill towards the beach. She drove straight down to the field gate. Tom was there in his land rover waiting for her, as was Aled who lived just up the lane.

"Where is it now?" asked Caroline, choosing to ignore the fact that Tom was pale and disturbed.

. . .

"I lost sight of it," Paul responded, looking around himself like a fully trained commando. Clearly anxious, and with reason.

"It went towards the bank of trees between your field and the beach café and little park area. I drove the tractor to the land rover and swapped, I phoned Aled here for some moral support, he told me about the murder in the woods too, had you heard?"

"Good God no," exclaimed James who had by now hobbled across to join them. They both listened as Aled went through the news again, they were both shocked.

"We haven't heard anything about this, and it's only up the road from us too, in fact, I walk through those woods fairly regularly with the dogs, to check on the horses, saves driving all the way around when the tide is right in, that is just awful, and here too, we never have things like this happening in this area."

The distraction had almost made them forget the reason they were all standing there. Caroline, took the gun off James and held her hand out for some cartridges, she opened the gun and loaded both barrels, then placed the open gun over the crook of her arm.

"Come on then," she indicated with a nod towards Tom and Aled. "You stay here, you won't be able to move quickly enough if anything happens", she said to James, telling him to wait for the police. Tom and Aled opened the gate and went ahead of Caroline, across the first section of field. "Where did you see it first? Let's go and see if there is anything obvious around there", said Caroline. Tom seemed a little hesitant to lead the way, the three of them on high alert for sight and sound of this creature that had been seen.

Even Tom was somewhat doubting his own eyes. They reached the tree that Tom had said it was spraying against, Caroline immediately bent down to smell the rough bark, she had no qualms about this, she said as she regularly smelt mares on her little stud farm, being able to tell if the mare was in season or not and ready for the stallion. Just a bit of useless information that the men likely did not really want to know. She spent a minute or so smelling before announcing.

"Yep, cat pee smell, I suppose it would be wouldn't it?" Tom and Aled were standing behind her, beady eyes looking around as if expecting to be pounced on any minute. "Come on, let's go to where you think you saw it," said Caroline again, indicating with the gun towards the woodland, prowling along cautiously looking to any person that came upon the strange scene as if she had kidnapped both men. They crept slowly ahead, Tom leading the way, both men looking ahead and to each side whilst Caroline bought up the rear.

"Do these things climb trees?"

Both men stopped in their tracks.

"Shit," said Aled, "Never thought of that!" They continued walking like SAS officers through the undergrowth, but terrified lest they actually saw it.

"It could be less than ten feet away from us in all this bramble and bracken," said Tom, adding almost as an afterthought, "In fact Caroline, you swap places and you go first."

. . .

"Why, are you scared?" she demanded.

"Well if truth be told, I'm more scared of you shooting me in the arse, if you think you have seen anything," he responded with a hint of humour.

"Fair comment," she said, simultaneously looking up and seeing a helicopter circling ahead. "Who is that?" she indicated towards the helicopter with her head, but not once taking her eyes off the ground ahead of her.

"Looks like the local police helicopter," said Aled, who would through his coastguard work be familiar with that type of aircraft.

"Hello," shouted a voice, "Hello," it was coming from back by the gate, but it wasn't James. They turned around, having been defeated anyway by the thickening undergrowth and the thought that this creature whatever it was, may well be watching them from above in a tree. They strode across towards the gate, coming to meet a policeman in uniform. Caroline was a little conscious of the fact that she was actually carrying a twelve- bore shotgun, though the policeman totally ignored it. After all it was James who had the license not Caroline.

"Good afternoon, I've come to ask you to step back now and return to the gate, I'm the Police Wildlife Crime Officer for the area, I believe you think you have seen a big cat?" Caroline sensed Tom Bristle as he said.

. . .

"I don't think I've seen a big cat; I know I've seen it; it was huge, dark brown- black, and bigger than a Labrador dog."

"More than likely that what you have seen is a fully grown male badger," added the officer.

"You are having a laugh arent you?" stated Tom looking shocked, disbelief and despair, obvious to see. He appeared to stand taller, he was offended at the insinuation that he was either lying or just imagining things.

"I know the difference between a badger and a cat, and in all my years living here, I have never seen a badger, dead or alive, I'm aware there are some up towards Holyhead, but have never heard of any over here. Anyway, badgers don't spray up trees and have a tail that can reach way up behind them." The officer seemed to totally ignore his response, having clearly made up his mind that only he could possibly be correct.

The cars at the gate had been joined now by another four by four, out of this came Iorwerth Davies and another two guys who both carried cased guns over their shoulders. How on earth had they heard of this thought Aled, the grapevine hereabouts was amazing.

"Hang on," called the Officer as he noticed them. He headed off towards Iorwerth and his mates and following whatever he had said to them, they got back in the car and drove off, displaying a definite thumbs up through the back-passenger window towards Caroline. The officer came back.

. . .

"The helicopter has picked up something on their FLIR camera, so I would ask you now to leave whatever it is alone, as its far more likely as I said, to be a badger." Caroline had already taken a dislike to the man, he appeared to be arrogant, but in her opinion, had no idea about wildlife. "What's a FLIR camera?" asked Tom as he turned towards Aled.

"It's just what they call the heat seeking camera they have on board the helicopter."

"So, what now?" asked Caroline as she went through the gate and stood next to James who had been talking to the three men.

"The tall bloke with Iorwerth lives near Penmon, he claims that he will come back late at night, he has infra-red sights and a silencer on his rifle, though I'm not sure really how I actually feel about them shooting whatever it is."

"No, I agree, but on the other hand I don't want any of my horses attacked, or any people for that matter, mind you I really hope they don't shoot one of our horses by mistake either," said Caroline. "Nor one of my ewes," shouted Aled across. Tom and Aled were standing together chatting, James joined them. "Iorwerth told me that he knows there has been a big cat around for a while, but no one believes him, he saw it one night crossing the main road out of the village towards Beaumaris, in the headlights of his car, jumped the walls he said as If the stone wall wasn't even there, then crossed the road in about two strides, but that was months ago according to him."

. . .

"Do you reckon he did?" asked Aled, "Maybe he had his beer goggles on, doesn't he like his pint?"

"He does," said Tom, he always has a couple in the pub on an evening, but I've never seen him really bladdered and I've never seen him getting into his car, he always walks home. Doesn't a hard working man deserve a couple of pints? Anyway, whatever I saw, is now either well gone or it's laying low, I will have a look on line when I get home, to see if I can recognise anything similar to what I saw."

Caroline and James got back in the car, said their goodbyes and thank yous, reminding the two men to contact them if they saw anything like it again. They promised they would.

Jo, Aled's wife had by then come down to join them, their little Jack Russel bitch tucked under her arm. They exchanged hello's and left the men to walk to their respective homes. Caroline drove down the lane to the beach front and turned around in the first convenient space, choosing to have a drive around the mares in the top fields while they were there. Doing it now would save a trip out later on. All was well, most were sheltering from the flies under the canopy of a big old sycamore tree, which formed an umbrella above them, tucked up close against a rock outcrop. They stood nose to tail, lazily flicking their tails at each other. They were totally relaxed and quitely content, as Caroline walked amongst them scratching bottoms and the backs of ears, dependent on what end was presented to her first. This was mainly her little band of broodmares and this year's foals, only five, she rarely bred more than five foals a year. They would be weaned and bought home to the main yard towards the end of October, if the weather remained half decent, handled and then prepared for sale after Christmas, though there was actually very little handling to do, so used were they to being touched and scratched, and having their legs and feet handled during their daily visits by Caroline and her business partner Emma. Caroline walked back towards the gate. James had stayed in the vehicle, not really able to walk far these days, but was totally able to visit the stock when he ventured across the beach at low tide, in their scot-trac vehicle, a machine he had bought a few years previously, basically a cab and carrying area behind it which was built like a boat, it was tracked so could basically get everywhere, it was even designed to float like a boat with the tracks acting like paddles, though neither of them had been confident in its advanced age to test out this capability. James was able to pop along the beach, and around the other fields as and when he liked, and the horses were well used to his visit, normally with a few bales of hay and a sack of nuts in the back.

When they got back to the yard, she finished the afternoon tasks and fed the horses that were stabled, mainly their stallions and bought the ones indoors, that had been turned out earlier in the day. The horse job never ended, she would be out later that evening around nine o clock to top up haynet's and skip out any dung produced in the intervening hours, it also gave her a pre bedtime opportunity to check all was well with them, it was often the time of evening where a gut feeling or a little sign, would point out that a horse was maybe unwell or uncomfortable.

James had gone straight indoors to finish doing the dishes.

Chapter Seventeen

THE SOCO TEAM had been quite a time getting the man out of the tree in the forestry, as many photos as were needed had been taken, with the poor guy in situ, quite a large an amount of blood had actually been found once they started looking for it, it had spread downstream in a tiny rivulet, and a considerable amount of it was around the base of the tree and on the trunk. A major scuffle seemed to have taken place. A couple of discernible sets of footprints had been found, but more than likely the victim's own, the other, the young lady horse-riders. One set clearly walking into the area, and the other, walking out. More than anything, there were hoofed scuff marks cutting into the ground where the horse had apparently according to the witness, spun around, then galloped off towards home, cutting quite deep with its shod hooves into peaty ground, amongst the more solid outcrops of rock. The fire brigade had been called to assist with the removal, but even that was quite an effort with brainpower, ropes and pulleys, due to not being able to get a rescue unit anywhere near, the method was certainly less than pretty, thought Huws. The fire team had been chosen carefully by their superior, the more experienced ones, who may well have seen a few more nasty incidents than the younger members. They had been useful, to help stretcher the body back to the road where Jones the local undertaker was waiting with the black van.

"Second in less than a week, bad do," he said, very softly spoken as were most funeral directors he had met.

"Straight to Bangor again?"

"Yes please," answered Huws. "I will be following right on your tail." Huws left the scene and drove the short distance to the forest gate. Eric Mansell was there waiting to close the gate behind him. Huws wound down his window.

"There are others from the team still on scene and will need to get through later." "Yes, I will keep an eye out for them and open and close as needed, I will keep the gate shut because if I don't, we will have every Tom Dick and Harry wandering about in here, I can't stop them walking in though. Cars, I can stop cars." Huws had no doubt that this man could stop cars coming up the track, he wouldn't like to meet him on a dark night anywhere, but he seemed honest and straight enough.

"I will send someone over tomorrow to talk to Dawn," Huws added.

"I don't believe she has any more to say to you than she has already told you," he answered gruffly, already half way back into his car. Huws took the ten minutes it took him to drive to the community centre to think what his next steps might well be. Two murders in almost as many days and some human remains, with very little evidence to connect the three, but nothing could be discounted. He would have a bit more detail on the bones in a couple of days, but Emyr Rowlands had told him it may well not be that useful, they could likely age the bones, but less likely know how long it had been there. He knew also that some of his team were following up on leads on the scraps of clothing that were with him, contacting the manufacturers, to see if they could possibly get a bit of a clue as to when the clothing would have been manufactured and sold. They may know a bit more in a couple of days. That may well give confirmation that it actually was the man they suspected him to be. That might just allow them to shut the door on that case and give his parents closure.

He pushed open one of the double doors into the entrance foyer, then the second lot of doors into the main space of the room. There was a scuffling of chairs, anticipation in the air as they waited for more news on what was speculated to be a second murder.

"Do we have a serial killer in the area?" called one of the team from the back of the room.

"Let's not second guess about anything at the moment, but you have obviously been told about this second victim. I'm off to the morgue now, and as soon as I'm able I will be back with more details, but for the time being keep up with the work concerning Sarah Jones." He turned towards the door, but added.

"Parry, you come with me." Noticing his young officers face actually blanching. "Yes Sir," he answered as he pushed papers into a pile on his desk and shut down his laptop. Huws was already outside and in his car, when Parry emerged, he had managed to just find a parking space outside, too early for the pub goers to have arrived as yet.

"Sorry Sir, just needed a pee before we go."

Huws didn't have a lot to say on the way to Bangor, only twenty minutes or so away and over the bridge crossing the Strait, dependent on the traffic, though most of the volume of traffic would be people coming home from work, from the mainland onto the island now, and he didn't think there would be any significant ferry traffic just then. He took the exit off the roundabout towards the hospital. On turning in to the carpark area he drove around the back. Parry had been particularly quiet during the journey, Huws suspected that he may, like himself not be the biggest fan of autopsies. Huws tried to put him at ease by saying.

"Look lad, I need you there, if only to take down some notes while I watch, no way will I remember everything that Rowlands has to say." This produced a bit of a thankful release of breath from his young sidekick, possibly feeling he could concentrate on the note-writing, as opposed to what was unfolding on the table in front of him. He had been to just a couple of them before, the one bit he absolutely hated was when they opened the skull to expose the brain with the bone saw, this part really turned his stomach. The rest of it he could cope with.

"Right," said Emyr Rowlands, sounding less bright than he had a tendency to be. "Let's get on with it shall we. Again, once Huws and Parry were seated in the viewing gallery, he drew back the shhet and started.

"Male, identified as a Mr Philip Morrison aged 51, address as per his ID in his wallet, driving license, bank card, RAC card, Cadnant gardens annual permit, as recorded on scene and in a bag over there". He directed a nod towards an evidence bag on the stainless steel table against the wall. The items would shortly be passed on to the forensic team to log. A complete picture of this mans recent life needed to be built.

"Found earlier today, hanging suspended on the branches of a pine tree in Pentraeth forest, a considerable amount of blood at scene due to exsanguination, following a catastrophic injury to the neck."

This is stuff that Huws knew already, a furtive glance at Parry saw him, head down busy writing in his pocket book, keeping his gaze very much away from what was going on behind the glass screen. Huws let him get on with it, very aware of how the young officer would be feeling at this moment. Jane the mortuary assistant was busy, photographing the body as directed, every angle, every mark and bruise. This continued for the next thirty minutes, samples were taken, organs were weighed and facts recorded as Rowlands continued with a running commentary throughout. Eventually, he nodded in their direction, behind the glass, as he turned away and directed Jane to undo his apron strings. He removed his gloves and left the room. Huws and Parry made their way towards the office and waited for Rowlands to reappear.

"What do we have then?" asked Huws as Rowlands sat down opposite him.

"OK let's just give you a bit of information first regards your skeleton, I'm afraid that we don't have a lot of information from the tests, other than it was a male, as we already knew, in his forties possibly and the nearest guestimate we can come up with, is that he could well have lain there for two years at least, maybe more. Does this match with anything you have come up with your end? We are also just awaiting results from a dental database search."

Huws nodded, most of this he knew just from the preliminary results. More than likely it was their listed missing person. Parry continued to write his notes, slightly pinker around the gills now than he had been fifteen minutes previously.

"Right," continued Rowlands. "What we have presented to us today, I would say most definitely ties in with our previous case only a matter of days ago, a brutal frenzied murder, a death caused by severe blood-loss, leading to a traumatic cardiac arrest.

From evidence at scene, the body was likely dragged up into the tree post-mortem, by I would imagine a system of ropes and pulleys, similar in fact to how he was taken down. I obviously have no real idea why someone would want to do such a thing. Some sort of ritual act maybe. He has severe lacerations to the neck, most of his neck structures having been ripped away, leaving his neck vertebrae exposed at the base of his skull, down as far as C6 which is virtually the whole of the length of his neck. X-ray results will confirm the fact that I found significant damage to the bone and multiple bone fractures. If he hadn't bled to death, he would no doubt have died due to damage at an upper level to his neural breathing control centre. Extensive bruising on the arms and upper torso shows a fair struggle took place, defence wounds more than likely, clothes torn.

"In my mind this is either a machete, or axe, but we need to put more work into our findings as yet. The torso in this case however was intact, all the organs were still in place and undamaged, so mainly head, neck and upper back area. Attacked from behind I would imagine. I don't think that with that degree of initial damage that he would have been able to put up much of a fight, poor sod. Whoever is doing this is quite possibly the most vicious killer I have come across, and that's saying something, having seen some fairly brutal murders in my time. I was involved on the periphery during the Peter Moore murders in the mid-nineties, he was a real twisted bastard. Between us we need to get this person behind bars as soon as we can, before you have another death on your hands. Whoever it is, I believe knows the area really well, and knows his way around the woodlands, knowing the places locally that not many people go to, but also, particularly in Sarah's case not going out of their way to cover their tracks, as in hide the bodies. It's almost as if they are out to get maximum shock effects."

Huws nodded his thanks. There was not a lot he could say. It was a disturbing case. Parry was still nose in his pocket notebook.

"You can stop writing now lad," said Huws. "Got all we need for now. Let's get back to base and give them the news, we need to step up now before this madman strikes again."

"Why madman and not a madwoman?" asked Parry.

"Good Point," answered Huws nodding his head vigorously, as he pulled the vape out of his pocket. People always said madman as opposed to mad women, although through history there had been women murderers as well, like Myra Hyndley, Beverley Allitt and of course Rose West, but it did seem to him in general, that women generally worked hand in hand with their husbands or boyfriends, all supposedly in the name of love, as opposed to be lone murderers. It made for an interesting discussion with his junior as they returned to the village hall.

Chapter Eighteen

IT WAS a beautiful early autumn day, a little nip in the air, but still some heat in the sun, the views from the yard were glorious. When Caroline and James first saw the smallholding one September day in ninety-three, they fell in love with it immediately, totally blanking out of their minds all the negatives that were likely to belong to it, and there would be lots. They were smitten. The house was small, but rooms could be knocked into one, a row of cowsheds were attached to the cottage which could obviously be made into useable stables, an old rusting Dutch barn could be replenished with a coat of paint, as could be cowshed below it. The fields fell away from the buildings towards the huge expanse of beach below, becoming progressively boggier the nearer the sea they got. There must have been a good fifty acres of swampland covered in bulrushes between their land and the sea, a conservation project maybe they thought, but over the years the reality was that it was impossible to rectify. Dreams of draining their land out into the swamp would never materialise, on finding that if they opened ditches it simply allowed the swamp to disgorge its sour brown waters onto their fields. Behind the cottage was the vast Pentraeth forestry, planted way back in the

Community Killing

fifties covering Mynydd Llwydiarth. This forestry gave shelter from all but the most direct northerly winds, a micro climate being formed in their protecting heights. The disadvantage however, that they had not initially been aware of was that the great forest blocked off any sunshine between November and March, the sun did not rise high enough in the sky for it to appear over the tall pines, permanently keeping the farm in its shadow. This would be the depressing truth through the winter months, something they had learnt to live with. They had between them built the stud farm up over the years, renting extra land as it grew and as it was needed.

On this particular day Caroline needed to take a couple of mares along the beach to the other parcel of land nearer the village. It was foal weaning time and the mares would be well out of earshot of the anxious whinnying foals. They were well handled, so she knew from previous experience that they would soon settle down. Her mother often helped her with tasks on the yard and would be more than capable of leading one of the mares along the beach.

Headcollars on, both mares were taken out of their stables with James on hand to shut the top doors, for fear of foals making a bid for freedom over the stable doors. Caroline and her mother set off down the drive, both mares neighing in response to the calls of their offspring. The route along the beach was a full mile and a half, but a lot shorter than taking the steep hill up to the village of Allt Goch, and down again to the beach along the road, risking traffic. As the mares feet touched the sand on the beach, the novelty of the feel of the soft sand caused them to promptly lose interest in the fading calls of their foals, they skittered playfully through puddles of receding sea water, the tide already well out. They took a shortcut over the saltings necessitating a few nimble jumps over the odd wellie sucking hole. The mares curling around the women, playfully jig jogging along, still well behaved and not pulling on the lead rope, very likely remembering about and anticipating the freedom of fresh fields. On this last matter they would be disappointed as Caroline always put them on relatively bare ground, for a couple of weeks post weaning to help dry up their milk flow, followed then by a move to fresh pasture to enjoy the last of the autumn grass before the winter months set in.

Today the mares would be put in the very fields that neighbour Tom had supposedly seen his black creature a few days before. Nothing seemed to have come of that, but she did suspect that Iorwerth and his mates may well have been around during the interim nights with their rifles and night sights. They were sensible country people though, and she was perfectly confident that they would not be doing the same once they knew that she had got some horses on the fields. She would however ring Iorwerth later just to give him the heads up. Her relaxed attitude was not from disbelief of Tom's sighting, it was just the hope that whatever it was had moved on somewhere else- someone else's problem.

The track off the beach was in sight, a sandy passageway with almost a naturally formed tunnel of bramble growth allowing them through. Just enough clearance for the mares to pass under. The brambles would soon die off as the winter settled in, in fact, she herself would clear some of them, with her regular trips along the beach during the winter months with big bales of hay for the out wintering horses, pushing her way through with the front loader and bale spike on her tractor. They emerged onto the lane, just a couple of hundred metres of lane now before they came to the field gates. From their left as if timed to the second, appeared James in the old Range Rover, who had driven up through the village ready to pick them up and drive them home to save the walk back. Caroline walked in front, her mare the strongest and boldest of the two, still jogging in anticipation of freedom, short memories clearly, foals totally forgotten.

Suddenly, the mare snorted and in straightening up allowed Caroline a clear view of the lane ahead. No more than two hundred metres ahead of them lay a huge big cat, its length including the tail taking up the whole width of the country lane, it was focused on something or other that was on the other side of the sparse hedge. Both women froze, her mother had seen it too, neither of them knew in that moment what to do. It was surreal. There it was, it could only be the exact same creature that Tom had seen not long

Community Killing

before. The mares stood head up like statues. Natural instinct telling them not to proceed. James, engine idling behind, from a slightly higher viewpoint, simply gazed out of the windscreen, as Caroline looked back to see if he had noticed. Obviously, he had, he was open-mouthed.

Stupidly, both women started walking towards it, dragging reluctant ponies behind them, Caroline was actually doubting what she was seeing, was it actually just a large dog? Maybe a figment of her imagination, something she was watching on television from the comfort of her sofa. She needed to just get a little closer. Her mother followed hesitatingly. Within seconds the cat got up onto it's feet, spared them a brief direct glance and without appearing at all threatening it turned tail and loped up the road, took a right, and jumped up a steep bank and off it went into a young plantation, but not without firstly pausing to take another look at the two women and horses walking slowly before him.

Caroline turned and looked at her mother, she returned the look but appeared speechless. James still bringing up the rear. His face expressionless, well at least not an expression that Caroline could read. This was most definitely what her neighbour Tom had seen, and although she had no real reason to doubt he was telling the truth, until you have seen things with your own eyes, you still can't believe what you have been told by a third party.

She called over her shoulder to James, walking backwards a few steps to check the bank again for fear the animal made a return.

"What do we do with these ponies, do we take them back home?"

"Only you can decide that", he shouted back through the window. "Most of the other horses are on the hill, I can't see much benefit in just taking these two home, I'm sure whatever it was will be well gone by now, don't you think?"

"Well gone?" shouted Caroline. "Do you reckon! It was a huge big cat, not a pussy cat, where the hell has it come from? Did you not see it properly?" She was getting scared now, the reality of what they had just seen sinking in.

"Of course, I saw it, but like you I have no idea where It's come from, so come on, get those mares up to the top fields instead of here at the bottom, and we will get home, I will ring a couple of people for advise when I get back."

Chapter Nineteen

IDRIS HUWS, stood outside the village hall, looking more like a fifty's youth than a Detective Inspector, leaning on the wall, one knee bent, foot up on the plasterwork. Vape in hand producing clouds of white vapour with every puff. The collar of his by now unfashionable mackintosh, pulled up against the increasing autumnal breeze. All he needed was for his thinning hair to be plastered down with brylcream and he would set the scene.

The village was placed quite high for an Anglesey location, catching the winds it seemed from whichever direction it blew, it got hard hit by winter snows as well from what he had been told, blowing straight across from the Carneddau Hills directly opposite almost, on the mainland. He hoped to god he wasn't still going to be here come winter. Lunchtime and evening business seemed to have picked up in the pub next door, since they had taken over the room at the start of the murder case, locals had kept away initially so maybe it was now by a case of the villagers having a nosey at what may be going on. He had spoken to the landlord a couple of times in the last couple of weeks, being a local councillor and on the

Coastguard team, Michael as he had invited Huws to call him, seemed to know most people in his area, but even he had drawn a blank as to any ideas he may have had which would lead them to the perpetrator. No one locally in his opinion had shown any traits that they would be capable of such thing. It was a close knit village, he was convinced but then again did people that were capable actually advertise or gloat about their abilities. Huws suddenly decided that despite his general dislike of visiting pubs whilst on duty that he may pop in later that evening, to see who was about, and have a chat with a few people, he certainly had nothing else solid to go on other than the fact they had received a positive identification regarding the remains in the quarry. The only queries that Emyr Rowlands had in that case, had been some deep scores on the femur bones, but the pathologist had eventually put that down to time and tide, and gnawing by animals. They had managed to get hair, and finger and toenail samples from the body, these however had given no indication as to the person having used drugs prior to death. Due to the fact that most of the flesh had gone, any other clues regarding how he may have committed suicide had drawn a blank. However, the parents would be able to give their son a burial, and as they say these days, get closure.

He pocketed the vape and headed indoors. Once through the double doors, the coldness of the room hit him, inefficient radiators heating up a poorly insulated high ceiling, most of the team wearing their coats. A couple had small fan heaters attached to extension leads placed directly under their tables. Their bodies desperate for a little warmth. One officer sitting on a blanket that he had then wrapped over his knees, Huws laughed to himself, he looked like a care home resident, fingerless gloves on his hands.

They sat at their makeshift desks, folding tables that would look more suited to a jubilee street celebrations, they were sitting on tubular framed sprung seat stacking chairs, more than likely now, considered 'Retro' or 'vintage', as his wife would call them, and as far as she would be concerned they could be quite valuable. Huws knew she would love to get her hands on some of these for her Etsy page to sell, she seemed to spend all her time sourcing stuff like this in her free time, storing things in every spare space in their house since she started her new hobby. She had mentioned more than once, her desire that once he had done his thirty years-service, that they would sell their suburban semi and buy somewhere with outbuildings, for her renovating and furniture selling. Mm, was all he could think of to say to that. He often wondered what he would do once he had retired, he was married to the job and had no hobbies or particular interest.

He looked at his team , heads down busy fingers tip-tapping away at their laptops, he watched them for a fair time, always intrigued at how they had such an ability to type on their keypads so quickly. Various wires had been set up running across the room to the various extension leads that were set up for the duration, he himself he was generally useless with modern technology, and watching some of the team bringing page after page of information, mostly police classified stuff up on their screens within seconds of a request, just totally baffled him, it made his brain hurt. He made sure that he never let them realise this.

No one had come up with anything as yet, not a single lead regarding the two cases. Sarah Jones and Philip Morrison still lay in a fridge in the local Morgue. Other than the similarity in their downright brutally inflicted injuries, they had made no headway in finding their killer, or indeed killers. He had been well taught by his seniors over the years to never presume the obvious. His team were still attempting to follow every single idea put in front of them, regarding people's movements around the time of both murders. Every local inhabitant had been spoken to, second home-owners had been checked out, cottage agents, had in some cases, reluctantly given out contact details of visitors, and self-catering cottage owners had given out contact details of their cleaners, to follow up on any possibilities that they may have found something unexpected. Only one cottage owner had announced that they had a strange couple staying with them at the time, who had left a disgusting mess, causing them to have had to postpone their next customers, to give them extra time to clean up. Traces of blood had been found resulting in a phone call to the police. A visit by SOCO found that it was in fact spilled red wine. Huws supposed that if someone chooses to rent out their property to total strangers, then you really have no idea whatsoever who they might be, and in some cases, what sort of mess they might leave behind. He sat quietly at his desk in the back room, he needed a bit of downtime to himself, he was in and out of the building so often that no one seemed to bother to notice his presence or absence. Certainly no one thought to switch on the wall heater. A quick look on his desk surface for any memos that needed his attention proved unnecessary, there were no papers needed signing, forwarding or authorising.

The clock on the wall said seven thirty pm, but it had said that every day since he had moved his team into the building, he looked at his watch, nearly 6pm. He would send most of the team home in a bit, totally pointless them freezing their butts off overnight, particularly as they were all contactable and didn't live a million miles away. One bobby on his night shift could come and check-up the building later on. In the meantime, he would scroll through the work to date on the laptop on his desk, maybe in the hope that something would jump out from the words in front of him. The ability to do that depended completely on his ability to find where the files were saved.

Chapter Twenty

IDRIS HUWS WALKED into the pub, the door opened and bought him straight into the main bar area, no inner hallway or porch. There appeared at a quick glance to be rooms leading off left and right. The air was fuggy, no doubt due to the large open fire at one end needing a sweep, causing warm smoke to hang in the rafters.

As soon as he walked in, as anticipated, the room fell silent. The few people at the bar suddenly finding something of great interest in the bottom of their pint glasses. He smiled to himself, it would always happen, he couldn't blame them, it reminded him of the old film Wicker man, when a police officer was sent to a lonely Scottish island, to investigate the disappearance of a child, and all the locals clammed up. He thought it may have been released in the early seventies, when he himself was probably too young to have watched it when first released. He remembered that it starred Edward Woodward.

"Good Evening DI Huws, what shall I get you?" asked Michael the landlord, breaking the silence. A welcoming tone to his voice silently serving as a warning to others who potentially might like to be less than friendly towards the Detective. "A pint of your best please", he answered and stepped across to an empty stool at the bar. He hoped that someone did not return from the lavatory and be displeased his chair had been claimed. Michael took a glass from the overhead shelf, checked it against the light and gave it an extra polish with his tea-towel. He recognised the chap sitting at the end of the bar sideways on, using the wall behind him to lean on. The man was doing his best to ignore his presence by making a point of looking away. This was the man whom he had spoken to outside the village hall, earlier on in the investigation, Iorwerth, if he remembered rightly, check shirt and flat cap, comfortable and at home in his surroundings.

"Good evening Iorwerth," he offered in his friendliest tone of voice. He didn't get what the answer was, it was so mumbled, in fact poor Iorwerth didn't look at all comfortable that he had been seemingly singled out for a conversation he looked a little aghast that a police officer might actually feel the need to speak with him. He stared into his beer glass.

"Are you keeping yourself busy at work Iorwerth?" attempted Idris Huws once more, he had no idea really what line of work the man was even in, but anything to start a conversation. No distinct answer was forthcoming other than a nod of the old man's head. Slightly disappointed that Iorwerth did not want to engage with him at all,he decided to turn away from him to allow the man to relax with his pint. The others that had been holding up the bar had slowly melted away, they found armchairs to sit on dotted around the rest of the room, they collected in little clusters. Far enough in their opinion not to be drawn into an unwanted conversation, but close enough to eavesdrop.

Huws reckoned there were as many women as men in the room, which was reasonably unusual at tea time in a village pub, but he did know by now ,that there were a few clubs that used the pub. Michael had been so kind as to fill him in on the regular weekly happenings under his roof. There would be amongst them members of community choirs and knitting groups, that had been usurped from the village hall, when they took it over and in one village worthy's vocal opinion infringed their rights to be there. The village

Community Killing

Chapel had been commandeered for the choirs purposes instead. This decision had not pleased everyone.

"Any developments on the awful incidents Sir?" asked Michael, as he passed him his beer. Huws, paused, he was not at all keen to divulge to the non-looking but listening customers at the bar, that all they had come up with so far, was a big fat zilch. He answered with a little doubt.

"We have a couple of leads that we are currently working on." Michael nodded and winked at him surreptitiously, his nod was aimed towards Iorwerth in the corner, though Iorwerth had his head down staring into his pint glass, which had just been refilled for him by another customer. Huws imagined it was quite likely, that a regular such as Iorwerth rarely paid for his pint, being well liked it seemed in the village meant a pint was automatically pulled for him when someone came through the door. Huws hoped he might initiate a chat with the old boy, but he wasn't holding his breath.

"Getting chillier now", said Huws, with a nod towards Iorwerth. Iorwerth looked up at him, you could almost hear his brain whirring as he nodded slowly, his rheumy blue eyes seeming to read right into Huws's soul.

"Yes." A pause.

"The smell of autumn soil is in the air now," he replied sagely, returning his gaze to the bottom of his pint glass. Huws noticed it was actually a glass tankard engraved with the old boy's name. He must be well thought of hereabouts. "Petrichor," mumbled Iorwerth,

"I beg your pardon?" reacted Huws. Iorwerth continued, "Petrichor, a word for the earthy aroma of rain falling onto dry summer earth." Huws just nodded, so surprised was he that the man had use a word, that he swore he had never ever come across in his life.

"Mm yes," more to show Iorwerth that he wasn't unfamiliar with the word.

"Did you hear about Endaf's yearling bullock?" asked Iorwerth, leaning forwards on his stool so he could lower his voice slightly. Huws straightened and stepped forward to hear.

"A bullock?" answered Huws.

"Yes, a young castrated male steer," he added.

"I know what a bullock is man, I meant, what about it." Huws immediately cursed his haste to criticise lest the old man clam up again.

"Endaf, along the beach, thought initially the other day that it had been stolen, it was missing from the herd, John that works for him had a wander all around the boundary, he soon found it due to the carrion crows, it was over a low wall on the seaward side of his land." He paused as if for dramatic effect. Michael butted in.

"I've heard about this sort of thing happening before, stock killed, butchered and the meat taken away in vans then sold, you hear of that being done in the north-west of England don't you, particularly with sheep, only the fleeces left in a pile complete with skins. It is sold on the black market to restaurants and suchlike." Michael had sidled up to Iorwerth in order to eavesdrop.

"No, absolutely no way," cut in Iorwerth. He argued vehemently.

"I picked it up from over the wall with my JCB front bucket and lifted it onto the knacker wagon, it had not been butchered properly, the flesh had been ripped off it, they clearly had a very blunt cleaver, it wasn't done by a trained person." He turned back to his pint, lifting it in Huws's direction, indicating a refill. Huws obliged. Iorwerth was deep in thought, shaking his head.

"Worth quite a bit too, a loss, a young steer like that." He nodded sagely.

"Did this Eifion report it to the police," asked Huws.

"Duw no, pointless really, it would probably take them a week to turn up to a call about a bullock," said Iorwerth, staring him straight in the eye, almost accusing him of police negligence, as if he himself was solely responsible for the entire North Wales Police force.

"Where will the carcase be now? Surely the insurers will want to send someone out to see it." Huws waited for the answer. The old boy looked thoughtful.

"Gaerwen incinerator, more than likely it will be ash, by now, cremated." Iorwerth slurped the last of his pint, wiped his mouth with the back of his hand and got up to leave. Huws glanced around, noticing that the group sitting directly behind him had clearly been awaiting a reaction, failing to observe one, they had gone back to their chatter and pints. As Iorwerth left with a touch to his cap, which Huws suspected may well be welded to his scalp, a group appeared at the door, chattering away, only to shut up immediately they noticed him at the bar. There you go, wicker man mentality again, he thought to himself with a wry smile. Around twelve people in all came in, most of them immediately bagging a table in either of the side rooms, clearly preparing to eat. Some hung around the bar and ordered drinks with Michael, well, actually they didn't order drinks, Michael knew them all and was familiar with their drink of choice. He briskly started filling glasses and passing them along the bar. Michael have noticed his interest.

"Local Community Choir members," he offered. "These are the regulars who take advantage of our Curry for a fiver night, you have kicked them out of the village hall where they usually gather, they have to go into the Chapel now , mind you by all accounts it is warmer in there." This was news that Huws was already aware of but his ears pricked up at the words Curry night, his wife Gwen had something on tonight, it was her Merched y Wawr group and she would probably be late home, by the time they had washed up the cups and saucers and put the world to rights and finished blethering.

"Can I order a curry please? Not anything too hot," he asked Michael, who nodded and shouted, "another Korma," through the serving hatch into the kitchen.

"Half and half?" With a nod, Huws decided to take himself through into the left-hand room, the fire appeared to have settled down now had settled now, there must have been more draw up the chimney, the smoky fug had lessened slightly. Its was one of the reasons why he and Gwen had chosen a log burner for their lounge, less smoke and ash mess. He found a small table in the front corner near the window, took his coat off and settled down with his pint. He had refused a second beer, choosing instead a pint of orange and lemonade to keep him occupied. A young waitress bought through his Curry, a shop-bought jar of Mango chutney besides the plate, cutlery rolled up in a paper napkin. No unnecessary finesse, which added pounds to the cost of a meal in any restaurant just a couple of miles away in Beaumaris, but he was pleased to find that the curry was well cooked, and tasty. He enjoyed people watching, when he was out and about, but it was never the same when people knew you were in the force, it would have been around the pub in an instance, people always minded what they said. He felt sadness sometimes these days, when he had joined the job policemen were respected, they were people to look to for help and advice. Nowadays sadly, they were looked upon as some sort of enemy, not in all quarters he understood, but by many. These good people of the village that were here this evening, he knew, would be disappointed at their seeming lack of progress, particularly on the young Sarah Jones case, she was one of them, a local. Poor Morrison on the other hand had been a relative newcomer, he hadn't really integrated himself into village life, so wasn't as well-known, not that anyone was less sympathetic. Huws could at this moment, guarantee that he and his team were being judged by the gathering in this hostelry. People were talking generally in whispers, the occasional raucous laugh erupting from the other room, only he knew, was because he wasn't in their room. This lot were behaving like a group of schoolchildren afraid of a telling off from a stern teacher. He realised he would be unlikely to gain any snippets of information in here. Pushing his plate away, and scrunching up the serviette he stood, grabbed his coat and prepared to leave. The bar room was fuller now, but the crowd parted like a pair of curtains to let him through. He knew that as soon as he closed the door, relief would flood through the punters. A fact driven home as he passed the windows of the room he had just left, and heard the same loud laughter as the other room, relief at his departure, a return to normality. He walked around the back of the pub to his car, the usual little group of smokers huddling underneath a wooden pergola festooned with finished hanging baskets, the fuschias hanging sadly needing deadheading. They watched his departure.

"Definitely wicker man," he smiled to himself.

Chapter Twenty-One

"HI CAROLINE", said Aled, anxiety clear in his voice, which surprised her as he was usually so laid back it seemed, about everything. He rarely had cause to phone her.

"Jo has just come in and said that your horses seem to be a little disturbed in your top field, she thought I ought to phone you and let you know. I will walk up the hill now and have a look, but maybe you should make your way over if you are not too busy."

"Thanks," said Caroline, already motioning James to get the car keys.

"We will come along the beach, the tide is out, we will be quicker. Thank you for letting us know." She stuck the phone in her back pocket, and grabbed at an old coat hanging in the utility as she went out through the back door. James was on her tail.

"What's up?" He made for the passenger seat, he was no fool, he knew Caroline would be in the driver's seat and off in a second if there was anything horsey kicking off.

"Probably nothing, but I'm a bit uncomfortable having seen the cat the other day. Jo reckons the horses are upset about something, Aled is off to have a look up the fields now. You said the lads had been keeping an eye out at night but hadn't seen anything though didn't you?"

"Yes, I did, they have been there the last couple of nights, they have night vision binoculars and all the kit, they haven't seen hide nor hair of anything at all, not a fox, or even a local tom cat. They actually said that it is strangely almost unnaturally quiet on the wildlife front, other than the horses mooching around."

"You do trust them not to accidentally shoot any of the horses, don't you?" Caroline had been a little wary of the men patrolling with guns, but she knew there was very little choice.

"Of course, they won't, they know what they are doing, they have grown up hunting and shooting and their fathers before them, they also know the area like the back of their hands. Apparently, they have been there from dusk till dawn for a couple of nights now and zilch."

"OK, if you trust them then I will trust them, you said they had silencers too on their guns, so it wouldn't frighten the horses if they did shoot something." James nodded. Caroline got to the bottom of the drive, and checking ahead briefly, she drove onto the beach through the cut in the dune, through the soft entrance mud onto the firmer sand, as she went straight out through a gap in the saltings, before bearing a right towards the east end of Red Wharf bay. They knew the beach well now, but still knew to just keep moving, the sand having the potential to be very soft in patches, capable of sucking down a static engine. Many a vehicle had become trapped despite all efforts, then covered by the incoming tide which was amazingly fast to rush in as the beach was so huge and flat. They crossed a number of small rivulets and were now driving along the edge of the saltings, which bordered the part of the beach that was usually busiest in the summer, mainly due to the awarding of a blue flag for cleanliness that it had. Thankfully it was not too busy on that day. Further along, the beach became more pebbly, giving way to a foreshore of stone. This is where she knew to keep to a certain angle, and drive off the beach to the tarmac road. They took a right and drove past Jean's beach café and the main car park before continuing on and up the hill. They passed by the entrance

Community Killing

to Aled and Jo's Bryn Gwyn Bach, and around the next corner past the usually empty second home opposite the entrance to their top fields. She pulled the car into the gateway off the road and got out, already scanning the tops of the fields and seeing the horses in a tight group. Before James had even got out of the car, Caroline was out and over the gate. Aled and Jo were already seemingly walking around the seaward boundary. Caroline had already done a head-count and come up with nine, instead of ten, there was a foal missing and clearly the little bunch of mares were upset. They were all watching Aled and Jo, but Caroline sensed the heads up, alert ears and occasional snort was caused by more than the strangers in their field. Caroline set off up the slope towards the bunch of mares, Aled and Jo turning back to follow her direction. Caroline counted again and a third time, definitely one foal missing. Boo the grey mare's foal, Boo was in a muck sweat, yellow sweat stains marking her silver neck. Hang on, she thought as she moved amongst them, sensing the mares were keeping their foals close. She knew that even though these were mares she had owned for a long time, in fact she had been at the birth of three of them, they could take fright in a second, one wrong move or sound. They were highly charged and on the alert. She could smell the sweat rising from their bodies. She could easily be trampled if they chose to take off.

Boo was injured, she was resting a hind leg, Caroline couldn't see an injury on her lower limb, but as her gaze travelled upwards, a huge open gouge down her flank from the croup down to the thigh was obvious, not one deep cut but three, that she could see from this side. This would need urgent attention. She moved around the back of the distressed mare, who was, she could see trembling, a mixture of injured shock and fear she guessed. There was a similar injury on her other quarter, this time also causing significant damage to her vulva and anus. A terrible thought crossed Caroline's mind as she shouted for James to phone the vet and bring a head collar and rope from the car. In the late eighties and early nineties, there had been a sick twisted and up to now uncaught person who was maiming and killing horses, by doing unspeakable things to them, in the south-east of England and East Anglia. Was this a similar thing? She certainly hoped not.

Aled, Jo and James got to her at the same time, James blowing slightly from the exertion.

"The vet is on his way," he gasped, handing her a head collar. "Shit, almighty," he exclaimed catching sight of the injuries. "How the hell did she do that? Has she been caught up somewhere."

"No idea," said Caroline, never one to cry but very close to bursting into tears.

"Her foal is missing too, it must have got through the fence somewhere, and she has tried and obviously failed to follow? Can you hear a foal shouting anywhere Jo?"

"No, we haven't heard or seen anything, we have walked the boundary and haven't seen any sign of it. Was it the pretty little bay speckly one?" asked Jo.

"I will go and have another look," said Aled, clearly not one for hanging around when he could be doing something more useful. "I will have a look on our side of the boundary too, you are welcome to bring the mare up to the farm yard for the vet to deal with if you like."

"Thanks Aled, but James will pop home in a minute and fetch the trailer, so once the vet has had an initial look here and maybe given her something for the pain, we will take her home, she will be happier there than somewhere unfamiliar where she will still hear her mates calling." Caroline was by now leading the bereft mare towards the top gate, the vet knew to bring his van to the pull in that James, minutes ago vacated. She would be happy standing by the gate with her friends nearby. They were starting to relax a little by now in the presence of familiar people, they were slowly following the led mare in a string across the paddock, foals all firmly pressed alongside their mother's flanks. The two older mares were still very alert to their surroundings and were keeping guard.

Dafydd Williams the vet pulled up in his van, mobile phone to his ear, the surgery telling him of some other emergency that needed his attention. He was always running himself ragged. He had been as quick as he could and luckily was at a nearby farm when the call came through. He pulled on his faded green overalls and opened the gate, with a nod of acknowledgement, never one for needless small talk and gossip. Caroline held the mare as Dafydd slipped his hand over her back, as he approached her quarters for fear of scaring her. He looked, then moved the mare's bloodied tail aside as he passed to her other side. The mare was getting cold now, and out of instinct and love for her animals, Caroline took off her jacket and placed it over the mare's loins for some warmth.

"Did you see anywhere the mare could have been caught up?" asked Dafydd.

"No, well I haven't looked but my neighbours here have had a look and the foal is still missing, we haven't found it anywhere, unless it's managed to get through somewhere and onto the hill. It's strange though that it isn't shouting because it's separated." Dafydd just nodded.

"Mm, these injuries are strange. I don't think they are wire injuries, these are equal scores down both sides and clearly its caught her vulva too, that is a nasty injury and I will need to debride it and freshen its edges a little so that I can stitch it up."

"James will be here in just a bit with the trailer to take her home, though most annoyingly but can't be helped, she is one of our only ones that hates travelling, loading her here might not be straightforward," said Caroline.

"I can give her some intravenous bute for the pain and just a small amount of sedative now then to settle her." Dafydd was always efficient and rarely had Caroline ever seen him panic, she knew that he would never take unnecessary risks, he always proceeded with caution and would, she knew, always ask someone superior if he had doubts. He had never let her down. Then Aled shouted from the other side of the hedge further down the hedgeline.

"It's here, I have found the foal, well sort of," he added. Caroline looked at Jo and asked her would she hold the mare for a minute. The mare standing quietly now, drowsy and slightly head down. Jo, was wary of anything bigger than a sheep, but she cautiously took hold of the lead-rope as Caroline set off at a sprint.

"I will shout if I need you down there Dafydd." James will be back any second to take over from Jo". Dafydd acknowledged with a nod, he was still busy examining the wounds, in his meticulous mind working out the best way to stitch it together. As Caroline reached the hedge, where she could just see Aled through its thickness, she asked him if it was OK or hurt. He replied that she may well not want to see the foal.

"I'm not squeamish, I've seen some pretty awful injuries over the years, with horses and other animals."

"Oh I can imagine, I'm sure you are not, but this isn't really something that you are likely to have seen before. See the bottom of the hedge where you are now, I reckon it got through there". She looked at a hole which she would have ordinarily have said was on a regular pathway for one of the many foxes that lived on the hillside.

"No way would a foal get through there?" she replied.

"No, I agree, unless it was already dead, and has been dragged through." Silence, the possibility dawning on her.

"The cat, that bloody big effing cat that we have seen." The thought of this was like a direct punch in her stomach. "You know something? Even though we have seen this cat, it's still like it happened in our imagination, and that we were somehow mistaken. Fucking hell, do you think the cat has killed it and attacked the mare, who was only probably trying to protect her foal? The bastard, the utter bloody bastard. What do we do now?" Aled had persuaded her not to come around to his side of the hedge, but said he would dispose of the remains, as they were. In fact, he told Caroline that all that remained of the foal was one hind quarter section. There was nothing else to be found, he did not want to have her seeing it for herself. This would be the stuff of nightmares for her for a fair while. Caroline returned to the top gate, James by now manoeuvring the trailer in the lane so it was up against one bank, lessening the chances of the mare evading entering the box, though he had noted that she was fairly dopey, needing great care on the journey home.

"Christ, you look as if you have seen a ghost," said James as he looked across at Caroline. He knew his wife was a tough cookie but she had clearly been crying. "We need to bring all these mares and foals' home so they are safer, that cat has killed and eaten most of the the foal." Dafydd raised his head.

"Cat?"

"Yes," said James, "A few of us saw what could only have been a big cat, just a few days ago. Im surprised you haven't heard already, in your line of work. We called the police and they sent a helicopter out with a heat-seeking device on it, and although it picked up something in the undergrowth behind the beach café, the Police wildlife liaison bloke was determined that what Tom next door saw was a badger, but since then we have both seen it, Caroline and myself and my mother-in-law. We saw it as clear as you are standing here now."

"One of the old boys that Aled sees in the pub swears he has seen it too, he says he caught sight of it crossing the main road towards Beaumaris in the headlights of his car, he and his shooting buddies have been out looking for it at night," added Jo. Dafydd shook his head in disbelief.

"I don't know what to say. I have obviously heard all sorts of stories hereabouts, but always assumed people were mistaken, but, I will say that these injuries on Boo, are indeed compatible with the sort of injuries, I would imagine a big cat would inflict by jumping on the mare's quarters. Caroline and James, you take the mare home, just go slow with her around those bends at the top, I will have a look over there with Aled, and I will follow you on. Put her in an empty clean stable for now with no bedding and just get some buckets of warm water ready for me, I can get to work on her straight away, the sooner the better."

Chapter Twenty-Two

DAFYDD WORKED his magic over the next couple of hours, intricate work, the mare deeply sedated but not enough that she couldn't remain on her feet, head down swaying slightly, though supported lightly on each side, by Caroline and Emma her business partner who had driven over at the speed of light once she had been told of the dreadful news. Dafydd freshened up the already drying edges of the wounds gently with a scalpel after an injection of local anaesthetic, in order to have live tissue to pull together. These sorts of wounds were always difficult to heal, post injury soft tissue swelling made stitches break down. Granulation tissue would very likely form. That would need to be dealt with again further down the line. Drain tubes inserted to allow for the residual pus, following almost inevitable infection, to drain away. Her vulva and rectum had almost become one gaping orifice, never the cleanest site to work with. They would need to fight this injury from inside and out. It would possibly put an end her ability to breed again. Whilst this was ongoing, Caroline had asked James to phone four of her horse-savvy friends, to come and help her fetch the remaining mares and foals from their present fields, and walk them along the beach to be closer to the yard. Thankfully this was a walk the mares were well-used to and were sensible enough to behave. They still had just enough time before the tide would totally cover the beach.

After Dafydd had finished his task, he left Caroline with a pile of antibiotic medication, and pain killing sachets of Bute. Boo, was settled on a deep clean bed and rugged up. The mare was extremely subdued after her horrific ordeal and the loss of her foal. As she was recovering from the sedative Caroline was saddened even more to hear the mares gentle whickers for her foal. Had she been a human, Caroline would have said that she was in that initial stage of deep grief after a huge loss. By the early evening, as the days were now getting shorter, all the broodmares and foals were at home in the front fields. Normally the bringing of the mares and foals' home, along the beach usually in later October for weaning, was a case of great jollity. Mares jogging along happily, foals who had spent a summer growing up as a little bunch of terrors, taking chances and doing individual high-tailed scoots along the beach, sometimes going way ahead of their mother, then suddenly noticing their solitary position in the middle of the vast beach, or spotting a distant human with a dog, to then hurtle back legs akimbo, lowering themselves to the ground in an uncoordinated galloping effort, to make an embarrassed return to the fold. This would happen many times on the stretch of sand between the top fields and the home farm, giving Caroline a chance to see which foals showed some promise regarding agility and bravery. Often she would try to hang on to a couple of lead ropes whilst at the same time catch a foals antics on her phone camera.

Today it was a more sombre affair, foals sticking close to their dams quarters, walking along the beach in a line, akin to a giant centipede, with interspersed large and small segments, the last foal bringing up the rear. They came off the beach through the cut in the dune and up the drive. Before Caroline had them led into the field underneath the cottage, she had a quick once over the mares and foals, for any other missed injuries but thankfully, none were to be found, the mares were released into the field. Caroline was glad that all her stock were now close by and easy to see. She could even see them from her bedroom window. Hopefully the dogs would alert her to any night time prowlers. They all put their heads down straight away, gorging on the grass, as if they had not relaxed to graze for quite a time.

Two days later, all hell let loose, the local paper had caught the story, there it was in black and white, a front-page headline with a half page on page three. "PAWS. Just as you thought it was safe to go on holiday". A headline with a photo of a snarling panther, page three headline was, 'Is there a Panther on the prowl' The full story was there, a police spokesman describing their search, and the involvement of the helicopter, the description of the injured mare. Caroline smiled to herself, another local horse owner had announced that her horse also had similar injuries, though when Caroline had previously warned her about the existence of a big cat, she had laughed. She did admit though, fair play to her, in the article, that she had thought Caroline was away with the fairies at the time. Their phone was on fire all day, though James dealt with it. Being a newspaper editor in a previous life before they met, this was right up his street. Caroline felt he was really just a little bit too enthusiastic, considering what was happening.

Caroline had checked Boo thoroughly that morning, she seemed fine in herself, but had refused point-blank to eat the medicated feed she had been given for her breakfast, Caroline had used her common sense and mixed the painkilling powder with warm water and given her that orally with a syringe. The antibiotic was more of an issue, but a phone call to the vet's surgery had prompted Dafydd to change the powders for an intramuscular daily injection, which Caroline was happy to do. She would fetch the necessities later from the local surgery when she had finished mucking out. A quick scan down across the field saw the mares and foals grazing in a huddle, one mare as is often the case, on lookout for predators, something that horses had never stopped doing despite domestication. Maybe they had been right all along, there were lions out there. It certainly seemed so. Caroline's mother who had taken an interest in helping with the horses, when she and her husband William, Caroline's father, had moved to live at the farm, finished up the morning yard work, with a last tidy of the muck heap. Emma, Caroline's business partner was off today, but was aware of what went on the previous day, having been one of the first people that James had contacted to come to help.

"Coffee", shouted James at the top of his voice through the front window. Caroline made her way indoors with her mother close behind, ready for a drink. On entering the cottage, the phone rang. James immediately answered, he appeared to be having an animated conversation about the cat. Caroline and her mother sat down with their coffee. James held the phone away from his ear, putting his palm over the mouthpiece. "The BBC wildlife person is on the phone, not David Attenborough obviously, he added with a half-smile, but the local guys from the BBC office in Bangor. He wants to come over this afternoon and have a chat with us. Is that OK with you?". "Well yes, I suppose it is", answered Caroline, realising probably for the first time, the enormity of what had actually happened.

Chapter Twenty-Three

"IFAN PUW," he said as he got out of the battered-looking old Skoda estate. "BBC Wildlife programme coordinator for Wales." He offered a hand, which James shook. He looked a very kind simple soul, bearded and a tad Bill Oddy-ish, thought Caroline. He wore a crinkled, well-worn and stained Barbour jacket and corduroy trousers, tucked into his colourful socks, disappearing into a pair of ancient-looking leather walking boots. Out of the other side of the car, the polar opposite of Ifan Puw emerged, tall lanky smartly dressed top to toe, a man in his sixties guessed Caroline, he was introduced as John Thompson.

"John here is a bit of an expert on wildlife tracking, his speciality being setting up infra-red cameras. We have caught film footage of many a British native creature with his help. We are rather hoping that you might allow us to place cameras in strategic positions, to see if we can catch sight of this big cat."

"Do you believe us then?" asked James. "The police seem to think it was a bit of a dramatic hoax, though the vet took some photos of the mares injuries before stitching them, and sent them to the big cat expert at Chester Zoo. They came back promptly to our surprise with the verdict that the injuries were compatible with what they would expect of a big cat, the police wildlife liaison officer however, tried to convince us when our neighbour saw it the first time, that it was a badger. Must be a bloody big badger is all I can say. I'm sure Caroline will show you the mare in a minute. We also have the remains of the foal, in a bag in the barn awaiting incineration."

"Of course, I believe you," he responded. "I've seen them myself, I hate to think how many big cats of different species are wandering the wilds of the United Kingdom. I've seen them myself, on the foothills of Cader Idris, near where I live, in fact there have been two there that I have seen together, though I have no idea whether they are male and female or the same sex. Time will tell on that score." Caroline, surprised herself, she was so pleased to hear this. She felt that no one would believe their bizarre sightings, certainly the police had made them feel like utter idiots.

"I'm so pleased you have seen it or indeed them, too, some people around here think I am mad, but you know, the people who have seen it around here, are very plausible sensible people, who would have no reason to fabricate the story. You will understand too, that a fox would certainly not devour a five-month-old foal bar one haunch." She was so relieved that someone was singing from the same hymn sheet.

"We were hoping that you could show us the whereabouts of the sightings. John can then choose, and decide the best places to put the cameras," added Ifan.

Caroline took to him straight away, maybe because of his slightly bedraggled Santa Clause, without a sack appearance.

"I can take you across to our other farm if you like, and show you where our neighbour Tom saw it first, and where mum, James and I saw it on the road, and where the mares were when Boo was attacked."

"Boo?" questioned John, having not uttered a word until now.

"Boo is the name we call the grey mare that was attacked," said, Caroline's mother, seemingly quite excited to get involved.

"Are we going there now?" asked Caroline, "I will just get my boots on if we are, and I'm warning you there is a huge acreage of wilderness between here and Aled's farm which borders ours. There is a network of old mine workings as well. It could be absolutely anywhere. I will show you all the likely pathways though."

The remainder of Caroline's long day was spent trudging through dense undergrowth, up hill, down dale, returning tired and muddied, declaring that she thought Ifan was going to have a heart attack, he was blowing so much going up the steep hills. They had however amid great excitement discovered paw prints that Ifan was certain belonged to a big cat and not a dog or a fox. He had filled the imprints with liquid silicone after photographing them, and returned to them an hour later where the casts had hardened into perfect pads. John had also discovered evidence of score marks, on the bark of a sapling, in the wetland area of land behind the beach café and car park, which he declared were at the right height for a stretching cat. This area was the first place that John placed a camera. High enough off the ground that a rabbit or fox or cat would not trigger the beam, but would certainly pick up and film a large wild cat. His little green boxes soon dotted the hillside, at points where the two men reckoned, may be on the pathways a cat may take. Cable tied simply onto branches and thinner sapling trunks. Time would tell they said, if they caught anything. John would be back weekly at least to check on them. "What do you think it actually is, and where would it have come from?" asked Caroline.

"As regards to actual cat species, I'm not a hundred percent certain. I've had a word with some big cat experts, and from the description you gave me now, I can go back to them and maybe get a slightly better idea, so tell me again exactly what you saw," said Ifan. He fumbled in his jacket and bought out a Dictaphone, the same type that James still had in his desk drawer from his newspaper days when he interviewed people.

"Well it was near as dammit black, but the sort of black our old lab goes when he is casting his coat, it takes on a slightly more brownish tinge, and it loses its shine. I would say, a bit like a horse at this time of year who loses that shiny gleam of summer, as its winter coat pushes through making it duller. It was much taller and lankier than Ben our Labrador, certainly longer and moved with a distinct feline action not a dog's. It was somehow slinking along, its shoulder blades prominent above its shoulders as if it was trying to make itself smaller, it's head was very much more cat like, but very strong features. The long tail drooped behind, almost as long as its body, the end of it slightly turning up. In fact it was virtually the width of the single track lane at the bottom of our fields when it was stretched out."

Caroline continued now, engulfed in her own enthusiasm.

"It was definitely feline, not a canine, everything about it shouted cat. It made absolutely no move to be threatening towards us, but actually looked at us for a fair few seconds before it lolloped up the lane, and onwards up the bank. The jump up the bank was effortless for it, and it covered the distance then, up the slope to the actual field in just a couple of strides."

"Wow," exclaimed Ifan. "You had that good a look at it?"

"Yes, and Tom next door will tell you the same I should imagine, he was really scared, being out there exposed on his tractor with no cab for protection. He was sat on his tractor when he saw it that first time, when the police came, he said it nonchalantly backed up to a tree down the bottom wet fields, and seemed to spray like a tom cat would, then walked away towards the bushes behind the beach café, but it certainly was no domestic tom cat," she continued barely taking a breath. "A lady along the beach had a horse of hers attacked as well, well at least now she thinks it was attacked, they thought it had been caught in wire a few weeks ago when it happened. Its fly rug was torn to shreds around its quarters and it had cuts there as well. Likely it would have been a lot worse if the rug hadn't been on it."

"Mm, may well indicate it is a juvenile then, an adult big cat would have no trouble flooring a horse, and at the end of the day, if you had something like an actual Black Panther in the area, you would have people going missing," said John. At this comment Caroline nearly choked on her words.

"We had two murders in the area a short while back in August, the police are still working on it, though by all accounts they are packing up their stuff at the moment and moving out of the village hall. Locals are saying they have only done half a job, they have still not got anyone for it. People are only just about starting to relax a bit again, hoping the perpetrator has left the area.

Do you think there is any chance at all that this could have been the cat? Richard and Margaret who live just up the hill from us said that the injuries were terrible on the young girl. Torn apart, from what Richard described to James. Richard was the one who found her it really upset him from what he told us at the time. And then there was my friend Dawn, she lives in the forestry, she found someone up a tree when she was out riding. She didn't actually see the man because she ran away and it was too high. Her horse threw her off, and she was hurt. Oh my God, what do you think?"

"Was that here in this village?" asked Ifan. "I had heard but being a mid-Wales man, I'm not that familiar with North Wales locations", he paused. "I think we need to ring the police, although I'm sure that they will have thought of this and made the link, surely they will have done, won't they?"

"Huh," butted in John. "Do you honestly think that they will link it. I'm sure I would, but you never know how much interaction you would get between a CID investigation and a Wildlife Liaison officer, who deals with sheep rustling and stolen osprey eggs and such like." Caroline drove them back along the beach, just so that they could see the vast expanse of wild untended acreage there was on the hillside, and that was without including the eighty-seven acres of forestry that covered the hill above Caroline and James's farm

Chapter Twenty-Four

WILLIAM EVANS SAT SLUMPED and dishevelled, on the worn horsehair-filled chair, by the fireplace, it had once been his mothers, she sat on it just like the Queen Mother, that she believed herself to be. Gaping holes in the faded material allowed the horsehair stuffing out of the armrests, antimacassars long gone. The armchair played host to a wonderful variety of insects along with the inevitable fleas that inhabited the sitting room in general, there were no other useable chairs in the room, most of them as they had broken, thrown out onto a bonfire. Mice often scurried across the floor, the rats keeping themselves more out of sight. Yellowing wallpaper hung in festoons off the damp walls, looking like some sort of macabre Christmas decoration. The line of damp growing ever higher on the wall to meet the dado rail. Sad Victorian faces looked out through dulled glass frames on the few old family photographs that his mother had hung up. He had never taken any interest in them and they had remained there as far as he could remember for the whole of his life. The damp from the walls gave the room a sickly sweet smell that he no longer noticed, but should anyone have entered the house, it would have turned their stomach. The wall above the fireplace was blackened by years of open fires, each one lit struggling to deposit their acrid wet wood smoke up a blocked chimney. A mixture of brick plaster and crow's nests allowing just a finger of smoke to exit the house. Sometimes the smell made his eyes burn. In fact, he was probably immune to all the peculiar aromas and bacteria that surrounded his living space. His mother would be turning in her grave if she knew the state of her old home. He didn't really care. On occasion the stench would be added to by the particular smell that a decaying rat body could spread into the living space, having died a slow hungry death up somewhere in the attics or within the wooden partition walls. The smell would disappear as quickly as it had appeared. The carpet in the room had long ago been taken up and burnt, only the grime-stained black and red quarry tiles now showing. His mother's era in the house deleted from memory long ago.

The days were darkening outside though it made no real difference indoors, he couldn't see out at the best of times. Most of the house windows had broken in turn to be replaced by a plastic animal feed bag, roughly nailed onto the frame. These would regularly be torn in the high winds and let in the cold air. October was peeping its autumnal head around the corner, the clock would go back at the end of the month, even now it was starting to darken at around seven thirty. He had no real thoughts on winter other than it might make his plans easier to carry out.

Winters however did increase his feelings of loneliness particularly as his last remaining sheepdog had died. He missed his dog. All his sheep had been sold. The local postman had, he suspected reported him for not feeding his sheep, nosy bugger that he was, no one else really ventured down the drive anymore. He rose from his chair which served now also as his bed, an old grey army blanket being used as a cover while he slept, but hardly easing the cold, which seeped through to his bones by the morning, being so threadbare and holey. He drew back the only remaining curtain from the

Community Killing

window and looked across the expanse of bay from his position high up on the hill. He sometimes imagined that the place might be worth a small fortune if he decided to sell, but he knew he never would.

He opened the old fridge door, it no longer actually functioned as a fridge. Along with his electric lights, it was turned off permanently since the electricity board switched off his supply for non-payment. He used the fridge now just to store the few tins of food that he bought from the village shop. He avoided shopping as much as he could. He avoided any interaction with people if he could help it. Oh, he was fully aware that quite a few people from the village had over the years since his mother had died, attempted to offer help, but it all wore away after a few attempts at friendliness when he continued to refuse the hand of generosity. He reckoned, they were only after any money that his mother may have had. He opened the can of beans with his pocket knife. Always kept sharp, devoured the contents hungrily and cold, then promptly threw the empty can onto the floor. The pile grew slowly until he shovelled them out into the yard when he was inclined to do so. Housework was never top of his agenda.

Grabbing a torch, he opened the back door which over the years had fallen into disrepair. The bottom section of wood, having rotted and softened and fallen away allowed the winter weather to run amok all around the house. He shone his torch ahead towards the woodshed, rats scurrying away, exposed by the light. Well used to their presence now, they ate any scraps thrown out of the door. They were the only living creatures who seemed to welcome his company. Gathering a couple of rain-soaked logs he threw them down in the entrance porch, and returned to the shed where his old dead car lived alongside his slightly less dilapidated Ford pickup, untaxed, uninsured. He topped up the generator at the back with petrol as it whirred and continued to throw out fumes. He glanced across and the red light was safely on at the bottom of the old rusting chest freezer. His only means of storing a bit of meat for the winter, though now his sheep had gone, there was a time when he used to butcher the odd one himself as needed, normally a sickly ewe, or indeed some he had found already dead. No point in wasting them. The freezer was running at just less than half full. It would take him through this winter though, he just needed to make sure it never ran out of petrol and thawed.

His old mother had taught him butchering skills, he was still quite a good shot, potting the occasional rabbit, had his shotgun licence not been withdrawn along with his twelve- bore shotgun. He was sad at that, it had been his father's, an old Purdey, one of the first over and under action shotguns designed in the early 1920's. His late father had been a good shot, joining in all the local estate, game- shoots, rubbing shoulders with the nobility. He died when William was just entering his teens, possibly the greatest loss of his life, no guiding hand, but his mother had taken over that mantle, she raised him like a little prince, and taken care of all the farm's business.

He returned to the house, as cold and damp inside as it was on the outside, lay a fire shredding an equally damp and old cattle feed bag, crumpled underneath a single log. The flame slowly took hold. He struggled onto his feet, wellington encased and sat on his chair, his body doing its best to suck the heat from the hearth before it disappeared upstairs and out of the holes in the roof. The rats were still he could just hear- having a party up there.

Chapter Twenty-Five

JAMES PUT the phone back onto its charging base, Caroline, and Emma stood in the kitchen, coffee mugs in hand. "What did he say?" enquired Caroline. "Well, at first he laughed, and was full of cocky bluster and police bullshit, but he listened fair play to him. I gave him both Tom and Aled's contact numbers. I added that Aled was an accountant and Tom a solicitor, as well as both being hobby farmers. This I hope indicated to him that they were trustworthy types with no reason to make up stories. I also gave him Dafydd the vet's number, so they could have a chat about the injuries. I did phone Dafydd earlier, to double-check that he was happy for me to give out their mobile numbers, all three had no issue with it. I'm not sure that he didn't think that we were all mad, but he had read the papers- he assured me he would have a word with the force Wildlife liaison officer, to see if he could find out which officers were on the ground the day Tom first saw it." James took a slurp of his now cooling coffee. He handed it to Caroline, "Can you just top this up with water from the kettle please, I can't abide cold coffee."

"And did he think that any of this had any relevance in the two murders?" asked Emma, in her own assumptions she did not feel the need to include the skeletal remains at the quarry, she felt they could not possibly be connected.

"Well no, I'm not sure he did think there was a connection, well at least he wasn't prepared in any way to admit it to me this morning."

Huws was back in his office, everything had been moved out of Allt Goch village Hall back into the comparative comfort of Llangefni police station. He took off his mackintosh, pleased he would not need to wear it in his decidedly plusher surroundings.

Huws was slightly disturbed at the contents of the phone call he had received less than an hour ago. Could he maybe dismiss it as tosh? He shook his head as he considered putting the information on the back boiler, the man had though been quite calm and very sure of what they had seen. People that he assumed would not make themselves look silly with such claims.

The investigating team were settling back into their glass divided offices, the comfort of superior technology all around them. Some of the more specialised members of the team had departed back to their own separate bases elsewhere to continue their work in their own highly specialized laboratories.

Work was still ongoing on the case, however his boss had ranted at him rather, the previous evening declaring that they were getting nowhere, not a single confirmed suspect despite costly investigations. Huws was annoyed that even things like this came down to money, these cases involved real people, real families, did that not matter at all? It wasn't even as if he had any loose ends he could tie up, nothing, zilch. The Wicker man mentality had defeated him.

His thoughts came back to the cat. It had come out of the blue, he admitted to himself that he initially laughed when the man was telling him about it, he was ready to dismiss it as a crank call, but the man had sounded calm and rather genial. Something at the back of his mind was nagging at him. A comment made weeks ago in the early days of the investigation, he wasn't sure that it hadn't been uttered, even before the second victim, Morrison had been found. Strange he thought, sometimes conversations from the recent past could just pop up in your headspace and have a more relevant meaning than had been recognised at the time.

Both the victims were still lying in a mortuary fridge. For the good of the family this needed to be bought to a conclusion.

The thought grew in his head like the workings of a giant computer, his brain stored every bit of information it had been told or seen, even if it had not struck him as important at the time, it would as sure as night turned to day, pop out to the forefront, usually in the dead of night when his brain refused to allow for restful sleep.

There it was, the old boy Iorwerth had said something, one simple sentence way back outside the pub, something on the lines of, 'No human has done this'. They may not have been his exact words but near as dammit. He needed to bring him in for a chat, or would that just cause him to clam up? No, he would venture into the pub this evening and hope the old boy was in his usual position at the bar.

Chapter Twenty-Six

IORWERTH WAS ENJOYING his second pint when the hush descended on the room and the policeman walked in. Little clusters immediately set up in various corners of the pub. Just the same as had happened the last time. What was it with some people?

Huws nodded at Michael, who grabbed a glass from the overhead rack in acknowledgment of his entry, he wiped it carefully with a tea towel before starting to fill it.

"Good evening Iorwerth," said Huws as he pulled a recently vacated bar stool closer to the old boy, still warm from the hastily removed bottom. "Can I have a word with you, strictly off the record?"

"Yes, I suppose so, but I don't know any more about anything since you last spoke to me", he answered gruffly, barely making eye contact.

. . .

"No, I fully appreciate that, but I want to ask you about this big cat that people claim is around." Iorwerth sat up at this comment, seemingly prepared to take more interest. However, he stepped down from his stool, and peeped around the doorframe behind him, then indicated to Huws that he should follow him through into the next room. Iorwerth made for a small round table in the far corner near the blaring television. He indicated that Huws should sit down. Huws pulled the chair towards him, he would much prefer to not have to fight against the television to hear what was being said at very little more than a whisper.

"Yes, there is one, I've seen it with my own eyes on the top road to Beaumaris, I was driving home late one night and it crossed the road in the light of my headlamps, huge it was. No point telling the authorities about it though, no one would believe you. Most of the people in this pub tonight would laugh at me."

"Are you often out late at night?" asked Huws. Iorwerth hesitated as if mulling the idea that maybe he should not admit to being out in the depth of the night. But he was never doing anything illegal, it was always paid work. Dispatching rabbits and foxes for local landowners. He continued, only after taking a deep draught of his pint.

"Well yes, particularly at this time of year, shooting you see, a couple of us shoot foxes, local farmers pay us per tail. This is the time of year the cubs are going on their own and they will do a lot of damage after Christmas come lambing time, and no doubt kill a few unsecured hens in the meantime." Iorwerth seemed to be relaxing, talking about a subject he understood.

. . .

"Have you come across any evidence that might point to the big cat having done some damage already in the area?"

"Well yes, I suppose so, it's difficult to be accurate because for instance, if an ewe lambs twins at night between the farmers checks, then likely a fox or indeed a cat will take one twin while the ewe is lambing the second, no one would ever know that one is missing, and I don't mean a domestic pussy cat either.

A better example would be Eifion's bullock or Caroline's foal. No fox would eat a whole carcase in one night whereas a Panther could do," said Iorwerth, getting pretty animated now. A subject of interest clearly.

"A panther?" exclaimed Huws, raising his eyebrows and backing off in surprise. "Really, what brings you to that conclusion?"

"Well my shooting mate is quite good on the internet stuff, I'm not, I am more of a reader. He looked it up after Eifion's bullock was found like that, first of all he thought it might be some melanistic, or something puma, apparently, that is a cross between a black panther and a beige puma and the offspring is black. There was a bloke quite a few years ago now, lived in Llangoed who was some sort of Professor at the University, he had big cats in cages in his back garden, had them for years, talk is locally that when you had to have a special license to keep animals like that, his wife had them released, it would mean lots of expense to put in new standard cages and provide decent runs for them and stuff. That was back in the mid-seventies though, I doubt those would still be around now, they don't live much longer than fifteen years in captivity, so I doubt it would still be around now having to fend for itself. They do have a territory of around 25 square miles though. Mind you if the originals were a puma and a panther and male and female, we could be looking at third fourth generation, but to go this long unseen? I doubt it."

Huws had to admit to himself that he had hugely underestimated the slightly scruffy individual sat across from him, he was no simpleton, far from it, he found a new respect for old Iorwerth. Gwen his wife had always accused him of being too quick to judge people, and treat everyone as a criminal until proven otherwise. He needed to heed her advice more often.

"I want to ask you, if you don't mind about a comment you made to me outside the pub a couple of days after Sarah Jones's body was found, do you remember?" He went on, "You said words to the effect of, no human could do that." Iorwerth nodded sagely taking a last dredge of his pint. Huws looked towards Michael and indicated another pint for the old boy.

"Yes, I remember, the first thing that came into my head when it got out in the village what the injuries had looked like, I thought big cat, even with the added exaggeration the description would have with every re-telling. When that poor man was found in the tree by the young lady from the forest, my shooting pals and I thought straight away that it would be the cat, a bloody big cat to drag someone up there." Huws sat head down, he had people to talk to, sooner rather than later.

"Thank you for your time Iorwerth, I truly appreciate you talking to me, it was most helpful and you have obviously done your homework on the subject. You be careful now when you are out shooting, you never know what you might meet."

"Oh, we have already met by torchlight. I knew it was the cat, bright yellow eyes, too far apart to be anything smaller, foxes and other animals tend to be a greenish or even a reddish shade when they reflect back at you. I had it in my sights," muttered Iorwerth sounding ever so slightly regretful.

"Why didn't you shoot it?" he asked. "Why would I? Everything has the right to live, but things have changed a bit since the two bodies were found, for whatever reason it has clearly started to stalk humans, that is why we are out at night. James down the road asked us to as well, after they lost the foal."

"Three bodies," corrected Huws. "This may well put a different perspective on the remains found at the quarry too."
"Yes, I can understand that," agreed Iorwerth.

Huws hoped to God that Emyr Rowlands had kept decent records of the autopsies, this changed a lot of things that had been believed as correct previously. He was confident he would have done his job as well as he always did. He was a stickler for records.

Chapter Twenty-Seven

ROWLANDS WASN'T best pleased to be receiving a call during a family celebratory meal. His family had arranged without his knowledge, a surprise birthday dinner. He was never one for parties, so a quiet restaurant meal had suited him.

"Can this not wait till morning Idris? Particularly as you don't seem to have another victim for me, I can appreciate your concern, but I'm sure it can wait."

"Yes, yes okay I agree." Huws accepted he was being just a tad exigent.

He placed the phone in his back pocket and sat at the table that Gwen had laid for his tea. Fair play to her, she had fully taken on the often-mad timetable of his job since he was promoted. No regular shift patterns now, but sometimes barely putting his head down whilst working a case, other than a quick snooze if he was lucky enough to have a comfy office chair, which in these last few weeks had certainly not been the case, in the chill of the village hall. Thank God he thought, he was working out of his normal office at the moment. Suppers were often reheated affairs in this house , but despite this she always made sure he was well-fed when he was there. She had less control of any rubbish he might consume in his hours of work.

"Any developments in these dreadful cases today, that you can tell me about?" asked Gwen. She knew full well that her husband rarely bought his work home. He never had. Very often the only way she found out about anything would be if she either heard any village gossip or she read it in the papers. Gossip was not normally something she was involved with, even in her monthly ladies' group or her weekly writing group, she would rarely be included in anything that people feared she may take home to her husband. Sometimes, being a Detective Inspector's wife was a burden, it put pressure on her as she was considered a worthy lady to open village fetes and such like. Always being invited onto some committee or other. She didn't mind this too much as it actually did give her some order in her life and regular happenings, the polar opposites to her home life with her husband.

Idris, exhaled forcibly, leaning back against the dining chair, he put his cutlery down and said "Uum, yes, well a cat, a big cat, we are slowly coming to the conclusion that an actual big wild cat has been responsible for what we thought were murders and a search for a possible serial killer, a bloody big fucking cat. Can you believe it."

"Hey, come on, no need for that language in this house." Gwen chided, Idris apologised.

. . .

Community Killing

"A few people have seen it and there have indeed been suspicious large animal losses which could be down to such a predator, or so the locals believe."

"Oh gosh the word predator is certainly scaring me, should I be afraid of taking the dog for a walk?"

"Lets not panic about things at the moment. There has been a bit of a cloak of secrecy around it, maybe for years I imagine, people scared of being laughed at and made to feel like their imagination has run wild. The first time it was seen in recent times, our force wildlife officer put the sighting down to it being a badger, the dingbat. All our work this last few weeks, if this is indeed the case, a total waste of time. No wonder we haven't come up with anything concrete. I'm not looking forwards to telling the Chief Inspector, he has been on my back regarding this case anyway as it is. He preaches all the usual, this is costing a lot of money and you have got nowhere speech." Gwen sat silent. She didn't know if she was more shocked by the cat aspect which sounded quite plausible, or sad that the case was clearly having such a negative effect on her husband, she was not aware that the Chief Inspector was pressurising him to this extent, but she supposed that there wasn't a bottomless purse for these things.

"How are you going to play it from now on?" she asked.

"I'm meeting Emyr tomorrow morning, Emyr Rowlands the pathologist. Do you remember him? Lovely chap, we met him during that concert in the Ganolfan?" Gwen nodded.

"He did the autopsies on the three victims. Well two, we had already declared on his say so that the skeletal remains at the quarry had more than likely been a suicide. We found the likely missing person through the database, all the facts correlated, mental health issues and so on, and he assumed as we did, that the body had been picked clean over time by carrion, foxes, domestic cats maybe, and then insect life and general decomposition in weather and tide. The family have buried him now. I really hope to god that Emyr has some decent photos and notes on the case, or we will be looking at exhuming his body and looking again. I don't want it to come to that for the family's sake, that would be terrible. Now, we have had such positive sightings of a likely big cat by some pretty sensible professional people who seem unlikely to make stuff up, we need to look at the other victims again to see if the actual reason for their death, could in fact be attributed to a big cat attack."

He continued, sounding exhausted, his supper cooling by the minute before him. "A fair few cameras, night vision, special ones, have been put up by some BBC wildlife people, so it will be interesting to see if anything comes of that. I'm also going to have to bring in all the people who claim to have seen it, so we can get individual statements regarding its description, then tomorrow, I will see about maybe talking to some big cat experts, Chester zoo, London Zoo, Longleat, anywhere really where we may speak with people who have expert knowledge regarding big cat behaviour. They may be able to point at what animal we are talking about and its likely further danger to the public and more importantly, how we can trap it. It worries me hugely that even if it has been around a while, it has now for whatever reason chosen to turn towards humans as prey. With winter virtually on top of us, it may get hungry and actually start tracking and stalking people. Look for instance, at the mile upon mile of remote footpaths we have in the area. On the coast and further inland, they have a huge territorial range apparently. It could well be comfortably wandering around the whole east side of Anglesey and possibly further west. Apparently, a jogger in Capel Gwyn, near Bryngwran now claims to have seen it, running alongside him on the other side of a wall, pacing him, step for step. Who knows, there may be other carcasses out there in areas where people never set foot. Oh Christ this does not bode well."

He picked up his cutlery and started on his supper, they ate in silence. It would be a restless night's sleep tonight.

Chapter Twenty-Eight

A FEW MINUTES TO NINE, Huws was waiting in the back office of the Mortuary suite. Rowlands swept past in a white-coated flurry followed by Jane his assistant, she had presided over the original autopsies. "Right, OK, let's see if I have got this right. Despite all our forensic tests and examinations, and hundreds of results, you have drawn no conclusions whatsoever that would give us a murderer in the case of these two victims?" asked Rowlands as Huws butted in.

"Three, this draws suspicions that the skeletal remains that were found in the quarry, is not as first thought, a suicide, it's now possibly linked to the other two." Rowlands looked at him over his glasses. "You think these victims may have met their unfortunate demise at the teeth and claws of a big cat? Are your superiors singing from the same hymn sheet?"

"No, not as yet, in fact this isn't open knowledge yet, I haven't approached the Chief with this new angle, I want you to have a second look at the two we still have here, to see if there could have been a possibility that the injuries had been caused by an animal, and hopefully you will have enough photos from the autopsy of the more decomposed victim whose body was released, and unfortunately maybe for us, buried. I'm sure you said something at the time, that there were deep unusual serrations on the femur bone, that was then put down to weathering due to exposure. Would you think maybe, they could have been inflicted by an animal such as a big cat, actually holding down a leg as it was gnawing?" Huws looked at his notebook again. "You said at the time, soft tissue tendon and muscle had decomposed completely and only fibrous ligamentous tissue held some of the bones together, particularly in the lower legs. Could that be because they were chewed off as opposed to decaying?" As such words were leaving his mouth, Huws felt as if he were in some surreal world, describing the sort of stuff that may only occur in the most bizarre of nightmares. He realised looking briefly from his notebook in Rowlands direction that the man standing in front of him , his glasses dropped to the end of his nose thought the same.

"But come on man, do you really believe this tosh? Grant you, the injuries inflicted were not normal, to what we would expect to see, but a big cat? Jane, put the kettle on please, we have some talking to do." Over the next two hours, every thread of possibility was discussed and double-checked, photos checked, autopsy details checked and finally as Huws had expected, and not looked forwards to, the two victim's bodies. The two bodies had at least been stored in a made for purpose forensic refrigerator. Huws even remembered Rowlands telling him a number of years before of this new hi-tec facility. This refrigerated room, allowed the body to be kept at a negative temperature, unlike the normal hospital mortuaries which were for shorter periods similar to a household fridge. The negative temperature although not freezing the bodies would certainly slow down the rate of decomposition.

Both bodies were coated in a light powder, its purpose Rowlands explained, to prevent any bacterial growths. They looked slightly gaunter, the skin having a certain sheen to it. Morrisons face was covered by a special sheet of skin-coloured plastic, which at least hid the horrendous damage that he had sustained.

Rowlands and Jane meticulously checked and double-checked it seems, every aspect of the initial autopsies against a computer screen on the wall, which not only gave an enlarged view of what they were seeing, but at a touch of a button in Jane's hand, previously taken photographs and numerical graphs and result tables appeared.

The conclusion was finally drawn, over a coffee, that Rowlands did indeed agree that the cause of death could well be a big cat attack. He agreed to put his professional good reputation and name on the line by signing a declaration saying so. "Do you remember the drink you had and vomited out, immediately after the first autopsy in this case? Well as long as you promise not to waste a good tot of Lagavulin, I will get you another." He poured out three measures, Jane once again, like on the previous occasion, joining them once she had cleared the tables and replaced the bodies respectfully, one above the other on their shelves in the fridges. "What do we do now?" uttered Huws.

"Well, man that isn't really a question for me is it. I'm happy to give a cause of death as likely caused by an animal, but proof? In all honesty you likely need proof, I'm not at all sure how you are going to get that, until you actually get a big cat's body in front of you for all to see."

"There are men out looking every night, but I'm not sure how long that will carry on for before the novelty wears off, and if you knew the area where it has been seen, then it's like looking for a needle in the proverbial haystack. One old boy that I have spoken to has had it in the sights of it's gun but didn't see reason to shoot it. There is bound to be a reaction from the anti-hunting brigade. The distance between the victim in the tree and the quarry is probably three miles as the crow flies, with the young girl's body somewhere in the middle. But their range is huge. I had a chat very early this morning before I came here with the big cat curator from Chester Zoo. He didn't seem surprised to hear of the cat, saying that it was known that there were probably, over a hundred big cats roaming in the countryside in the UK, maybe even more, along with Wallabies, Racoons, American mink and Parakeets, most having escaped from captivity, and mostly denied, from fear of repercussions, for illegal owners. It was a big thing at one time for owners of stately homes to own lions and tigers. Most of these however were handed over to zoo's when the laws changed. He also said, and this is the worrying thing. It's likely old or injured, one or the other will mean it is unable to stalk normal prey, which it would have been doing, lambs, rabbits, ground-nesting birds, cats, small dogs if given the opportunity, but being older and less efficient a hunter, may have led it to be hungry. They don't eat daily, in the wild they may eat a deer, or wild boar a week, between those as a snack, they may eat smaller things like armadillos in the wild. However, being a poor hunter may well mean it is turning its sights to easier prey. A healthy adult cat would never purposely be seen by us, they are just too secretive for that he reasoned. Here on Anglesey for instance, no walker would expect to come across a big cat on a public footpath through the woods. However, in his expert opinion, and he sounded totally plausible you could in fact walk as close as ten feet away, from a well hidden big cat, and have absolutely no idea that it was there. It also explains the types of injuries inflicted both in the initial kill, and in how the kill was devoured. The cat may well have been disturbed he assumed, when it killed the male victim hence it dragged him up into a tree. An easy task apparently for a creature such as a Panther. The only other animals who could do that would likely be Lions or Tigers, particularly of the Sumatran variety who are known to stalk their potential victims, sometimes for days at a time, singling out an individual in remote villages. Siberian Tigers were also pretty big. The description given though, points towards a Panther."

"Shit," said Jane who had joined them at the beginning of this description. "I won't be walking in the woods anytime soon, I'm out walking every chance I get!"

It was a very subdued Huws, that walked back into his office at lunchtime. No matter what way he tried to play it in his head, he was going to have to tell his team that Sarah Jones, Philip Morrison and the lad from Barmouth had more than likely been attacked, killed and partially eaten by a big cat. But tell them he did. He had entered the incident room and rapped a desk with a pen, everyone looked up expectantly. Within seconds you could have heard a pin drop in the room such was the reaction, until one young CID rookie laughed out loud.

"Are you having a laugh Sir? A big Cat, surely the locals have had one too many magic mushrooms at a party, and come up with a fairy story. All the work we have put in, all the house to house investigations, the phone calls to every man and his dog, we will be a laughing stock." Huws let him have his rant and watched as others clearly agreed with him, all nodding their heads. He passed a memory stick to Pc Howard,

"Can you put this up on the screen?" Happy to pass on any potential IT use to his team. Within minutes autopsy photographs appeared on the screen of all three victims. Huws for the next hour laboriously went through them, notebook in hand, filling them all in on Rowlands' comments and opinions which could very well tie these up with a cat attack.

"Right, next job, while I go and talk to the Chief and try to persuade him that what we have found is plausible, I want you to go through each and every search case on Anglesey in the last five, no ten years, and tie up autopsy cases to any bodies that were found, see if there are any possibilities that any others could actually have been killed in the same way. It's unlikely, as the Zoo bloke feels this is the result of an old or injured animal, but we want to cover all the bases. Also, I want you to get onto a guy called John Thompson, here is his number." Huws wrote the number on a scrap of paper and passed it to a still dumbfounded WPC. "Ask him to check his wildlife cameras that they set up. I know it's only a couple of days or not even that, but they have been up overnight now at least, and if the animal is still in the area of its latest kill, they may have picked it up on one of the cameras."

Huws was on a roll now, having gone from not having a clue what he was going to say, to having plans coming out of him like post vindaloo diarrhoea.

"One of you contact the Daily post, they did a story on this a few days ago, we need to now confirm that we, as the Police, come up with a response to this situation without making ourselves look like a load of numpties and scaremongerers. We need to get a press release out which asks people to be vigilant, preferably not going out alone to anywhere remote, and to be careful and aware of their immediate surroundings. I'm going to ask if we can have the helicopter up a few times with its FLIR device, to see if it can pick up anything remotely panther like in the area of Wern y Wylan, the Pentraeth forestry behind, and the woodland between Wern and Allt Goch which is a vast area. Maybe a sweep around the quarries along the coast towards Penmon too, though apparently there aren't as many places to hide. Cave rescue hopefully if I can persuade them to, considering they may come face to face with a big cat, will have an explore in the caves, of the old mines between Wern woods, and Allt Goch". "Wow, fancy going into a cave and coming across a panther," said a voice from the back. Papers were shuffled, phones were dialled, Huws, left the room and prepared for his chat with the Chief. This will be fun, he thought as he straightened his tie.

Chapter Twenty-Nine

AUTUMN MOVED INEVITABLY INTO WINTER. The Chief Inspector had almost choked on his tea, when Huws suggested that the murders were actually caused by a wild cat. Rowlands the pathologist had confirmed, that indeed having looked again with a totally different mindset, his conclusions were that the damage could have been, and very likely had been, caused by a large predator, in this case the black cat which had been seen.

The case was closed as far as the police were concerned. Relatives, although aghast initially at the conclusion, had accepted it and had been allowed to put their loved ones to rest. Life went on. Anglesey, became a hive of big cat activity, every man and his dog had seen it. Rhosneigr, Dulas, Parys Mountain, Capel Gwyn, Newborough, the hills around Llanfairynghornwy, you name it, it had been seen there. The worrying aspect was that a couple of people claimed to have seen two. Research on the subject claimed that a cat in captivity might if it were lucky, survive for twenty years, however a cat released into an environment such as onto the island, would more than likely live for closer to eight to twelve years if it wasn't captured or shot. It gave the game shooting enthusiasts something totally different to hunt over the winter months. The zoo experts were worried about this aspect, worrying that a glance-off shot, as opposed to a kill, might in fact render an animal less capable of hunting, therefore making it hungrier and more likely to take another chance at a human. Some people who had first hand sightings of it slightly changed their life patterns, Caroline and James were now very wary of using some of their hillier landlocked fields, bordering Wern woods. Dawn up in the forestry, stuck to the open tracks whilst hacking out, rather than veering off into the darker corners of the woods. Mountain bike enthusiasts were now tending to seek the thrill of the forestry tracks in groups, as opposed to alone, and generally the local farmers were more aware that they may have more than a fox to worry about.

Obviously, there were still the sceptics, but woe betide anyone in the local pub who tried to belittle Iorwerth and his sightings. He had become a little bit of a celebrity in the retelling of his story to anyone who asked. In fact, the whole thing seemed to have created a little group of believers who lived in a slightly surreal parallel world to everyone else, they spoke of the cat amongst each other but chose not to openly discuss it for fear of being ridiculed.

The one person who in fact had anything like proof from that winter was Caroline, the only person with an actual photo, taken through her kitchen window when she had been washing up, an actual picture of the cat crossing a short bridge over a ditch in their back field, casually, as if it had all the time in the world. The photograph had been sent to a big cat expert, and verified to be a melanistic puma, likely full grown and elderly. By its coat which lacked a healthy lustre, it likely was not managing to hunt efficiently as suspected, hence why it had stalked humans. Whether it was a temporary blip and it had recovered from sickness of some sort, would probably never be known until it was captured dead or alive.

However, Caroline had an even more frightening encounter with it in the late winter, after the killings when she was woken from sleep to hear the horses noisily whinnying and banging their stable doors. She ventured out in wellie boots and dressing-gown to check, lest one of the animals was colicing, only to encounter the big cat standing sideways on, no more than fifteen feet or so away from her. Random advise gleaned from watching a Sir David Attenborough TV programme, regarding encounters with Grizzly bears in the wild, led her to raise her hands in the air, stand on tip toes and slowly retreat backwards. Make yourself look big he said, being only five foot three that was quite a challenge, and she couldn't remember whether she was supposed to maintain eye contact or not.

The cat made no indication that it was going to attack. She was rescued from the feed-room shortly afterwards by her father and sister, who lived in part of the property, armed with coal shovels, banging the sides of the shed as they approached. Clearly the sight of Caroline in her dressing-gown had been too much for it. No sign of it was seen, even after casting the strong light of a big torch down over the fields below.

Winter became spring, the village and Anglesey in general slipped back into its normal rhythms, people started walking the footpaths and lanes of the area once more, alone and in groups. The sceptics having already forgotten and some believing the police negligent and foolhardy, to have closed what they believed to be a murder case with the guilty party still likely to be on the loose, and maybe local, people putting blame on the weirder inhabitants of the locality, the loners and the unsociables.

Community Killing

• • •

Character traits like this were always picked up on in rural communities, where everyone reckoned to know everyone's business. Maybe someone waiting on the next opportunity. Only time would tell.

Chapter Thirty

THE COASTGUARD SERVICE continued to have call-outs and training sessions, the inevitable searches for missing persons, one of the less pleasurable tasks asked of the teams. People would always be going missing, it was the nature of human beings, things happened to them within family circles, marriage breakdowns, mental health issues, drug and alcohol abuse and dependency, and as had probably always been, and poorly recognised, post-traumatic stress disorder, a condition still not receiving the attention it should have.

Some people were never found, some people never wanted to be found. They were added by the police to the missing persons database as failed finds, friends and loved ones destined to a life of hope that one day they would be found alive, or even dead, that, at least gave closure. The team local to Allt Goch had for a time, been a little cautious if the search was centred around the so called big cats territory, but nothing suspicious arose to make them think there was any animal involvement, however Ceri refused point-blank to search anywhere unless there were at least two of her buddies with her, and tended to be the noisiest coastguard on the team, in order, she claimed to frighten a cat away. Tomos though reckoned that any big cat would take one look at a feisty Ceri and would not dare attack her.

Their search methods of sweeping ahead with a torch, left and right, and then behind themselves to cover the track from another perspective, always made Ceri nervous just in-case she was being followed, stalked, but she was quite confident that if Tomos released one of his regular and totally toxic farts, it would instantly kill the cat.

In the position of Coastguard volunteer, you needed a sense of humour and be well-used to banter. It was after all sometimes the only way you could deal with the things you saw in the job.

Pub life carried on, the choir had been allowed back into their village hall, the various chess, dog training, knitting, and reading clubs had slipped back into their routines like feet into old slippers at the end of a long day.

Chapter Thirty-One

WILLIAM EVANS in his own grumpy way enjoyed the spring. It wasn't quite the same now that his sheep had gone, but it did allow him to catch a few more rabbits for the pots. He used the old-fashioned snare method, knowing full well it was considered cruel and an old-fashioned method, but he checked the snares two to three times a day, the rabbits never suffering for long before he dispatched them, he would though feel inordinately cruel when he found a doe in the snare who was in milk, understanding that the kits would most likely, at this time of year, slowly starve, and perish inside their burrows. He would skin and quarter them and add them to whatever he happened to have stewing in the pot on the fire.

The only aspect of the spring that he didn't like, was the increase in backpacked strangers that crossed his land. They had the perfect right to- he knew that full well, there were mapped public footpaths, but he still saw it as an intrusion on his privacy. He had never understood the need by some people to trudge around the countryside, particularly crossing what was obviously private farmed land, disturbing stock and making farmers feel the need to be careful as to what they grazed in a particular field, particularly bulls. In his opinion, though bulls were often less harmful than a field of newly calved cows, they could give anyone a run for their money protecting their calves.

His mother had never minded, in fact she had always left some scones or Bara-brith in a small open-fronted shed by the gate, along with some eggs. There was an honesty box, it was quite surprising how much pin money she made in a good week. That was until some of the local youths actually cottoned on to a cash supply and started walking down the lane to steal the contents. This saddened his mother, who continued to put in her offerings for quite a while before disappointment caused her to give up. The shed still stood forlorn and dilapidated at the top of the drive, always empty now. He had no hens since the last bedraggled Rhode Island Red had died and he certainly was not inclined to cook scones any time soon.

William Evans had visited the local town the other day and although the odd person knew him and acknowledged him, it was certainly not a social visit, he had purchased a couple of loaves which he would chuck in the freezer in the shed, a few tins of beans to keep him going over the next week, and unusually for him, a few potatoes and a pot of granules to make some gravy. He listened in to chatter whilst he waited to pay in the queue, talk was of a local big cat which was now believed to be the guilty party in what had been thought to have been two, likely three deaths.

He was pleased to receive knowledge of this news. He could have told people years ago that the cat was about. Living where he did, it was a regular visitor which he had crossed paths with on numerous occasions. Choosing no longer to mow the fields the pastures had grown into tussocks of new growth over old for quite a while. Thigh high in places. Yellow ragwort making its way upwards and reseeding and spreading year-on-year as did the docks, nettles and Fat hen. Flattened tracks criss-crossed the fields, the regular motorways of foxes and on occasion this big cat. There were some flattened areas where an animal could have lain and rested. He had, in fact taken to throwing the odd rabbit into the field if his snares had captured a rabbit too many. Another wasteful act, and he supposed that he should in reality just put them in the freezer, for less fruitful times. He had never felt threatened by the cat, assuming that at one time in its life it had lived alongside humans albeit maybe in a secure cage.

It was an animal he was thankful for, the knowledge of its presence would now allow him to have a few more guilty pleasures in life, than he may have done since the time his dear old mother was alive. No point making a song and dance about it, until now it was unlikely anyone would have believed him. William Evans, a man of ursine build, largely ignored by the high class tourist brigade in town had a little more spring to his step as he made his way towards his battered old pickup truck.

He planned, when he got home to re-lay his fire and get it going well, he would place the old iron griddle wire across the heat once the fire had settled and died down, when satisfied with its heat, he would place the meat onto the griddle and cook it through, some for tonight with a baked potato and gravy, and if he was lucky it would last him a few days with a bit of bread.

This meat supply would last him through the year if he were lucky, he would then need to find another chance like the last one to take him through other years. He would need to be make sure he never got careless. The quarry was one of his local haunts, remote, quiet, though there was talk recently of adding it as a scenic route to the local section of the coastal path, bloody footpaths again. Rabbits bred by the dozen down there, that was the main reason he originally went down there, long before the big cat came on the scene.

The poor man that he encountered down there, just over two years ago didn't have a chance against him, being that he was a towering bear of a man. Bloody do-gooder townie, he had been sitting there off his head on whatever drugs he had taken. William was not wise to the drug-addicted ways of some of the world's population, he had no experience of alcohol either, his mother had always been vehemently against it, mainly due to her own father having killed himself through drink. The man actually had the cheek to start ranting at him for his cruelty. Dispatching rabbits was quick, as humane as he could make it, if there was such a thing as humane slaughter. He had even offered the bloke one to cook up on

Community Killing

the beach stones, loads of driftwood around he had suggested, but oh no, he just ranted about all creatures being equal, it was because of people like him, the man ranted who had absolutely no moral code, that the world had become as it was. William was quite naïve to these ways he referred to, not having a television or ever reading a paper. The only thing he read was his mothers old Bible but only very occasionally. Suddenly spittle covered William Evans' face as he was prodded and poked repeatedly in the chest by the stranger's forefinger. William stood his ground for a while in disbelief rather at the ranting. The rage continued, he involved God, and how Evans was clearly a disgrace before God for thinking he could willy-nilly kill creatures as he felt inclined. He then accused Evans of being an embarrassment to his mother.

It all happened in a flash, the penknife entered his neck just below the ear and cut towards the vulnerable centre of the neck, cutting across blood vessels which gurgled blood over and down the man's shirt collar. A look of disbelief and utter surprise, before the eyes emptied, a look that Evans reckoned he would never forget. The sense of power it gave him aroused him beyond belief. The man fell to his knees as if praying to the giant of a man before him, but he was already dead, when he slipped to the ground. William Evans looked around, knowing there would be no one to have viewed this atrocity but nevertheless.

He needed to think quickly. What would his mother do now? What a stupid thought, his mother would never have done such a thing, but she loved her son above all else, she would have a solution for this situation.

A plan came into Evans' warped mind in an instant.

He dragged the man up behind the old stone dressing sheds, roofless now but there were still a few concealed corners to carry out the next stage of his plan. Bleeding an animal is important after death or it taints the meat, he had a length of rope that he used to tie up the neck of the old hessian sack, that he carried his rabbits it. He tied the man's ankles together, then dragged him to the rusting metal framework of the shed where the brickwork had collapsed. His head thumping roughly over the pebbles and bigger rocks.

Evans knew it wouldn't be hurting him now. Throwing the end of the rope over a beam; he had checked it held his own weight by hanging off it. With difficulty and a lot of grunting, he tied the mans ankles together and Evans started to pull the weight equivalent he reckoned, of a well-grown two-month-old Hereford bull calf. The man hung by his feet in a grizzly upside-down hanging sort of position. Williams assumed that even though he was already dead, and that his heart would have stopped beating, just like a Sunday dinner cockerel he would drip out his life blood, or like the pigs that had been hung in the old sheds. Blood, then valued, and saved for the preparation of black pudding, every part of the pig used. He would aim to do the same. No waste. His mother had been in the habit of presenting a cold unfinished previous meal in front of him, should he leave food on his plate. It took him two days to cut him up into joints, he left the arms and the head, three separate journeys did he make, up and down the hill and across the fields mainly by the light of the moon, returning home to his freezer like a sinister Father Christmas without the hat and beard. Between visits, he had covered the body in a sack, to prevent attack by birds and foxes, though he suspected that the rats may well have had a nibble through the night.

Task completed. He had stripped the meat off the bone, keeping the skeleton intact, he had even re-dressed the man. He was then cut down and placed just behind the building, a nightmare vision in empty jeans and shirt. A rictus grin, jaw dropped, already hollowing cheeks looking back at him, half shut empty eye almost staring in judgemental disbelief. The other eye had clearly provided a meal for a scavenging carrion crow. This vision he imagined would live with him for a long time.

At home by candlelight, he had rolled up the meat from the legs, the abdomen and the back, creating what he believed looked very similar to rolled joints expertly tied by a butcher, all skills taught to him as a young boy by his mother. Surplus strips of meat he had put through the old mincer. In his mother's day, given a surplus of intestinal tissue, the mince would have created reams of sausages. He would have to make do with mince. He had not been able to

Community Killing

strip the arms, he felt slightly sick at the thought of the skin still having the sleeve of tattoos on it, he couldn't use that.

The barely hidden remains had eventually been discovered as it transpired years later, he had in fact enjoyed the proceeds of his cleverness on many an evening, before the two kayakers had found the man, all scraps of remaining flesh by then, disintegrated and eaten by various creatures. Just a partly clothed sun and wind-bleached grinning skeleton remained, still the same grin, a few ligaments still hanging on like gnarled yellow ropes. He knew this, because over the period of time since the dispatch and the discovery he had silently walked down to the quarry to monitor the level of decomposition, in fact he had found the whole process fascinating.

It was quite amusing to William Evans, to hear that the man had indeed been identified, and like the other two genuine cat killings the other side of the village, this was believed to have been the same.

Unfortunately, for William Evans, his frozen meat supply was going to eventually come to an end.

He was no longer too worried about this, after all, the cat was still around, as were the damned nuisance ramblers. He would very likely get his chance again, he had killed once, surely, it couldn't be that difficult, to do it again.

Facts on Fiction

This book has been written by a woman, who has had many personal sightings on her own land, and local area of a big cat, as have her neighbours and friends. Her theory is that the only way it could be there, is that a captive wild cat, has at some time been released and adapted itself to living wild. It has not in reality harmed anyone, unlike the Cat in this book. That is a pure figment of the authors imagination as is the twist in the 'tail'. Only time would tell on that score. The locals in general will know of the sightings, some adamant in their descriptions, others sceptical.

The village the book is based on is a place that sprawls along a vast wooded hillside, its western end covered in a forest, hundreds of acres of neglected wild land, criss-crossed by pathways and tracks. The lower parts of the village spreads out onto ten square miles of beach.

Woodlands hide a network of ancient caves, blocked by and large old mine workings, semi-hidden by self-seeded sycamore saplings.

Facts on Fiction

The authors smallholding was at the centre of the length of the beach, one of the primary locations of the actual sightings. The horse attacks are real, as is the loss of the bullock, clearly the human attacks are a work of fiction.

Years have passed now since the last sighting in the area, however at the time of publishing, there was a recent sighting more to the east of the island. If it's the same cat that was seen in the early two thousands, it will be a very old cat by now. It is hoped that there are not more on the island. The BBC wildlife camera side is real, cameras were set up. The newspaper reports at the time are also real as is the only photograph that was taken of the animal.

The author hopes that whatever its demise, or in fact if it still alive, that it has had a happy existence on our beautiful island.

About the Author

The author lives on the island of Anglesey off North Wales, her interests are the outdoors, walking the coast and hills. She was previously a college lecturer and a Coach and examiner for The British Horse Society. She now Trains people in First Aid Skills and has been an Active Coastguard volunteer for 23 years to date.

Her main love was her horse breeding business alongside her late husband and business partner, being one of the few Artificial Insemination Technicians at the time in the area. She now spends her time teaching, looking after her remaining geriatric brood mares and rescue hens, and turning out when her pager goes off, whilst dreaming of writing novels on jaunts in the campervan.

We can all dream.

She has drawn on her experiences of many aspects of life to write this book. Her previous published works have been mainly equestrian journalism and a children's story 'On the Run' also about the Cat.

Acknowledgments

This book is fiction based on fact, which will make itself apparent as the tale develops. All names used are fictional but most places do exist. People may well imagine they recognise themselves in the story and I thank all the people who were actually involved alongside me in the true parts of the tale; my parents and sister and business partner who also witnessed various scenes from this book. Also huge thanks must go to my step-grandaughter Hayley, yet again, for helping me with the more technical aspects of book publishing.

Also by Anne Roberts

DI Huws Book 2 Community Secrets and Lies

DI Huws Book 3 Community Confessions

On the Run- a stand alone short story

Printed in Great Britain
by Amazon